TANNER

THE BURNETT BRIDES

BOOK SIX

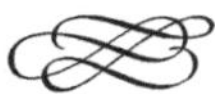

SYLVIA MCDANIEL

Can A Matchmaking Ghost Heal Two Broken Hearts?

Tanner Burnett served his country well in the Iraq War. Now he's returned home with a badass case of post-traumatic challenges. The least little noise has him taking cover. So when a ghost starts talking to him, he thinks she's just another PTSD hallucination.

After graduating culinary school in Boulder, Colorado, Emily Young became the newest rising star in the world of the culinary arts. Yet, two years after her husband's death, his memory still haunts her. Needing a fresh start, she takes a job at the Burnett Ranch in Texas.

Only problem...she has a one-night stand with a man she meets in a hotel bar, later to learn he's her new boss. Can a matchmaking ghost bring two lost souls, who never intend to marry, together and heal them?

Can One Night of Passion Cook Up a Forever Love?

The Burnett Brides Historical Series

The Rancher Takes A Bride

The Outlaw Takes A Bride

The Marshal Takes A Bride

The Christmas Bride

Boxed Set

Burnett Brides Contemporary Times

Travis

Tanner

Tucker

Joshua

Jacob

Justin

Cameron

Caleb

Cody

Desiree

Burnett Brides Contemporary Box Set Books 5-7

Burnett Brides Contemporary Box Set 8-10

Burnett Brides Contemporary Box Set 11-14

Copyright

Published by Virtual Bookseller, LLC

Cover Art by Dar Albert
Edited by Tina Winograd
ebook ISBN 978-1-950858-81-1
Paperback ISBN 978-1-950858-82-8

❀ Formatted with Vellum

CHAPTER 1

The Texas sun beat down on Emily Young as she lay out beside the hotel swimming pool in a new two-piece suit that fit her slim body. No one told her about the drastic weight loss plan grieving caused. With sorrow, pounds just melted away.

It had been years since she'd taken some time to relax and enjoy herself, and starting tomorrow, once again, she would be tied to a job in a new location with new people surrounding her and a town that didn't know of her past.

This time it would be far away from the memories that plagued her. Memories that were heart-wrenching and left her in tears.

This time she was starting over in a new state. But today and tonight were her time to relax and rejuvenate. To rest and prepare for her new adventure. To adjust to the summer heat.

She'd traveled a long way to get to this hotel and spend today preparing mentally for her new home in a state where the temperatures soared in the summertime and there was no snow in the winter. A state where she knew no one and they didn't know her past.

And yet here she lay beside the hotel pool relaxing. Today had been wonderful. All about her, and yet she still felt anxious about her new job and new beginning. Hopefully those feelings would disappear with time.

A tall muscular man dove into the pool, the splashing water cooling her off, filling the air with the smell of chlorine. How long had it been since she'd felt a man's arms around her? Too long. How long since a man had kissed her? Too long.

She watched as he swam the length of the pool, his muscles rippling as he moved through the water with purpose. Each stroke was a powerful push as he swam across the pool.

Not bad. Not bad at all. Actually a nice welcome sight. One she had not enjoyed in a long time.

Finally, he surfaced and shook his head sending water droplets flying from his dark hair, then he turned, glanced at her, and smiled.

They were the only two at the pool. The sun would be setting in a little over an hour and most of the families had already deserted the area. They were alone. And yet she didn't fear him, but rather enjoyed gazing at him.

"Good evening, ma'am," he said.

"Good evening," she said. "I have yet to reach *ma'am* status. That's for old ladies and I'm not there yet. Though the sun feels like it's hotter than a Fourth of July firecracker and baking me right into old age."

He grinned, his full lips spread wide with perfect white teeth making his smile brilliant.

"Sorry, I was taught *ma'am* was a show of respect."

"Respect for someone older," she said. "Don't push me there."

"Never," he said. "Are you from around here?"

"No," she said. "I'm just passing through on my way to a job."

"It's always this hot this time of year," he said, swimming to the wall nearest her. His muscular arms held him up on the side of the pool.

An instant sizzle of heat spiraled through her as she stared into his emerald eyes with long, wet, dark lashes. A trim mustache covered his upper full lip and she had the most incredible urge to taste his lips. How would they feel against hers?

His arms were tanned, his biceps large, his chest ripped with muscles and his abdomen had the nicest six pack she'd seen in ages.

Oh, dear who had taken over her body? She didn't react to men like this. It just never happened. And yet it had been years since she'd been attracted to a man or even noticed the other sex.

One good thing had already happened since she'd come to Texas. This rugged, handsome man had reawakened all her lady parts. They had come out of the deep freeze and were once again on high alert, warming at the sight of him rather nicely.

His smile seemed to delve straight into her soul and she almost gasped.

Licking her lips, she smiled at him, trying to remember how a woman acted when a man was flirting with her. Did women her age still flirt?

Oh, come on, she wasn't that old. Mid-twenties, but she felt like she'd lived a lifetime.

"I like hot," she responded, her voice giving a soft laugh.

"Good," he paused. "You're in the right place. Where are you from?"

"Boulder, Colorado," she said, missing the mountains, but not the memories. Missing the cooler air, but not the pain of her past.

"No wonder you like it hot," he said. "Tanner Smith."

"Emily Wilder," she said, not giving him her full real name, but rather her maiden name and wondering why. But she was new to the area. About to start a new job, and she didn't want to be found. Not by anyone.

Her family was gone and John...

The past needed to stay behind in Colorado.

"Nice to meet you, Emily," the man drawled, his deep voice sending delicious trembles down her spine. It was like his voice touched her every nerve. Like he reawakened her sleeping libido. It was still alive.

"Where are you from?"

"Born and raised a Texan," he said, leaning on the edge of the pool and gazing up at her with those deliciously enticing green eyes that seemed to want to remove her bathing suit.

And strangely, she wanted to let him. She didn't know this man. She had not desired a man in so long, she'd forgotten what the feelings were like.

"Here in Granbury?"

"No," he said. "My family owns a ranch a couple of hours from here."

There must be a lot of ranches here in the area and he wasn't telling her where or the name of their spread. Oh well, it didn't matter. She was not looking for a long, lasting relationship. That was not in the cards for her.

One would last her a lifetime.

"Would you like to go to dinner with me?" he asked. "I mean we just met, but I'm really tired of my own company and would love to have some female companionship."

He was a stranger. She didn't know him. And yet, she felt such a strong attraction to him, and it was the first time since John she'd even thought about another man. The first time in so long and she was determined to start her life over here in Texas. To be stronger. To begin life again.

To release her bonds and live again.

"Yes, but could we have dinner here at the hotel restaurant? I'm uncomfortable getting in a car with a stranger and going to dinner."

He smiled. "Of course. Actually, that's what I had in mind. That way I can get up early in the morning and head home."

That made her feel more at ease. While she was stepping out on a limb here, she wasn't quite ready to give him all her trust. She wasn't ready to hop into bed with a total stranger and yet, she was very attracted to him.

Plus, she, too, had to leave fairly early in the morning to arrive at her new job site on time. A nice dinner with a man and then she'd be in the room by ten and asleep by eleven.

"What time?" she asked, wondering about this man she had agreed to take a leap of faith with.

It was the first time in seven years she was going on a date. The memory of her first date with John flooded her senses and she pushed the thoughts away. No, just no. She was beginning a new life.

"How about eight?" he asked. "That gives us ninety minutes to clean up."

She'd spent the afternoon going through her cookbooks, planning her first week on the job, and the dinners she would prepare. So she was ready to begin when she met her employer.

"Yes, that works," she said. "I'll meet you in the bar."

That way, she could keep her anonymity without giving him her room number.

The man smiled, his full lips looked soft and tempting and were such a contrast to his rugged face. There was something about him that drew her.

"See you there," he said.

As he swam off, she wondered if she was crazy. Meeting a man at the swimming pool and then agreeing to go to dinner with him, she'd never done anything so brazen, so bold, in her life and yet she was glad.

This was the new Emily. The courageous, brash, and strong woman who had put the past behind her and was now moving on.

"To Texas," she said to herself softly. "And new beginnings."

CHAPTER 2

The moment Tanner saw her, he knew she was the one he wanted to connect with. To finally blow the soot out of his sex engine. The last time he experienced lying in a woman's arms had been before he left for Iraq five years ago. Five long, dusty years of trying to put that god-awful war behind him.

Five years of reliving every battle he thought he would die in. All the artillery fire, the exploding of mortars, the crackle of his radio telling him help from the air was on the way while he thought he was going to die.

He only hoped and prayed that tonight his PTSD took a hiatus and let him have a good time. He only hoped that this woman, Emily, would give him the honor of having sex with him.

Sure, it was a lot to ask and he was not normally into one-night stands, but he also knew he would never subject his trauma to a permanent relationship. He was broken, and until he felt certain that he was healed, he would never marry.

No woman should have to put up with a man who fought almost a nightly battle. Or at least one every few days. There was no rhyme or reason to when they appeared. Only, suddenly, he was spiraling back in time, fighting a battle once again for his life.

Regardless of what anyone told him, he was not fit for "forever after" or even longer than one night.

Glancing at the clock, he slipped his billfold into his jeans and put in a couple of condoms. More than one, praying for two, ecstatic if they used three, hoping that tonight, they would do it more than once.

What if she told him no?

Then he would return home still yearning for a woman's touch. The feel of her arms as she clasped them around his neck and her sweet moans in his ear.

No, he would never resort to paying for a woman, but he hoped that tonight, he and Emily could find satisfaction in each other's arms. Maybe she was just as lonely as him and wanted the same thing.

He'd seen no wedding band. No outward signs of commitment. He would never get involved with someone married. Not even for a one-night stand. They were off-limits.

The woman was beautiful and when he'd seen her blonde hair and soft blue eyes gazing at him, he'd known. She was the one.

Rubbing on cologne, he checked the creases in his jeans making certain they lined up with his boots, made certain his shirt was tucked all nice and neat in his pants and he'd removed the stubble from his chin.

At this moment, he couldn't wait to get her back upstairs and explore every inch of her luscious body. Her soft lips, her bountiful breasts, and that tiny waist his hands could probably reach around.

If he was looking for a relationship, she'd be on his radar, but he knew that was impossible. Until he found some kind of help that would end his episodes of war, he would never commit to anyone.

With a sigh, he knew it was time. Tucking his hotel key in his shirt pocket, he glanced around the room one last time.

One last test of his breath and he was ready to go.

Whatever room they chose, he wanted her to see he was a neat freak and that he was prepared to pull out early in the morning.

Time to go back to work.

Closing the door, he hurried down the hall and got on the elevator. In a matter of seconds, he was on the ground floor.

He saw her sitting at the bar, in a summer dress with strappy sandals on her feet. Slowly she sipped on a drink and he hoped she wouldn't get drunk. That would be a complete turnoff, because if and when they had sex, he wanted her fully functional to enjoy what was going on.

"Good evening, Emily," he said, walking up to the bar.

With relief, he noticed she was drinking a soda. Maybe there wouldn't be anything in it.

"What can I get for you, sir?"

"Water," he said.

Her brows raised.

"Normally, I don't drink."

"Good," she said. "I'm having a Coke to pick me up for the evening."

He grinned. He'd been right.

"Saw too much drinking in the military and it made me aware that people act stupid when they're drunk."

"I completely understand," she said.

Occasionally, he had an alcoholic drink, but most of the time, he drank water. Plus, he wanted to be functional tonight if they had sex. And he did not want his PTSD to act up. That would be so embarrassing with a stranger.

"Shall we find our table," he asked. "I made reservations."

She smiled and he took her hand to help her slide off the bar stool.

"Have you eaten here before?"

"Yes," he said. "I stop here occasionally when I have to go into Dallas."

This was where he spent the night when he was going to return from the VA hospital. Oftentimes, he needed some time to process what the doctor told him about his condition. Plus, he didn't like to drive late at night. Too many deer on the road.

"Your table is ready," the maître d' told them as he led them through the restaurant.

Most of the crowd was gone and there were only a few people remaining. He placed his hand on the small of her back as he guided her through the tables. It felt so good to touch a woman. To smell her sweet scent. To feel her soft skin.

And yet, he had lied to her this afternoon. He'd not given her his real name because of the notoriety of the Burnetts in the area. All he needed was for her to realize where he lived and seek him out.

It was better that tonight, no matter what happened, to be just about tonight and nothing else. There was no future in this relationship. No chance of anything past morning.

When they reached the table, he pulled out the chair for her.

"Thank you," she said, sitting.

"Would you like a glass of wine?" their waiter asked, walking up to the table.

"No, thanks," she said, and Tanner shook his head.

"I'd like a glass of sweet ice tea," she said and he nodded.

"Me too."

After the waiter walked off, they picked up their menus.

"What is good here?" she asked.

"Everything. I like to get their grilled steak," he said.

"Then that's what I'll have as well," she said, putting the menu down and smiling at him.

Those sparkly sapphire eyes had his heart pounding in his chest at the thought they could be sharing the night together. Her sweet full lips were a temptation he couldn't wait to kiss.

Reaching across the table, he took her hand. "It's been a long time since I was attracted to a woman."

She smiled. "So you're normally attracted to men?"

He threw back his head and laughed. "No. I'm just kind of picky regarding women."

"Good, I'm picky as well. The last time a man asked me to dinner was seven years ago."

Stunned, he stared at her.

"That's a long time."

"Yes, well, it was my husband," she said.

Oh, great she was married. But she had not been wearing a wedding ring.

"No, I'm no longer married," she said. "Things happen."

Great, she was divorced. Maybe it was best if he didn't ask her a lot of questions. The least amount he knew, the better.

"Any kids?"

"Oh, no," she said. "How about you?"

"No, I've never married," he said softly. "The war kind of ruined that for me."

For a moment, her face looked stricken and then she picked up her tea and took a big gulp.

"So what do you do?" she asked.

"I'm a ranch hand," he said. It wasn't entirely the truth, but close enough. It was best they stay off really personal topics. The least amount she knew, the better too.

"Do you take care of cattle and horses?"

"Yes," he said, thinking there was so much more to his job than just caring for the animals.

"Have you ever been in a rodeo?" she asked.

"Years ago," he said. "But now I'm too old and I just can't do it any longer."

"How about family? Do you have a lot?"

"More family than I can handle," he said. "Most of us live on our spread. It can get very involved, very quickly."

He laughed. If the Burnett's grew any larger, he feared they would have to buy another ranch. As it was, he expected his older brother Travis to announce his engagement any day, and his younger brother Tucker, the man's business was growing by leaps and bounds.

When those two married, there was still a whole passel of cousins that were single. And supposedly a matchmaking ghost who was finding them all their spouses. Well, he didn't believe in ghosts and she could find everyone else but him. He had no intentions of ever marrying, not while he suffered from this shit.

A band began to play in the bar. Sitting there across the table from her, it was all he could do to not just blurt out what he wanted from her. And if she agreed, to hell with food, they could just go to his room. But he knew that would probably send her running.

"Would you like to dance?"

A grin spread across her face. "I would love to."

They rose from their table and made their way to the dance floor where a slow two-step was in progress. She moved into his arms and he breathed deeply of her female essence.

A woman always smelled so good, and Emily was no exception. The smell of flowers and something soft had him closing his eyes, wondering what it would be like to be with her and hoping that he'd get lucky tonight.

Oh, it had been so long. And just holding her felt so

special. If only he could find someone to spend forever with. Someone who knew how to handle his episodes.

The feel of her in his arms, soft and moving against him, almost had him moaning.

This was what he needed. And hopefully after dinner, she would agree.

The music ended and they moved apart.

"Thank you," he said. "It's been so long and that was great."

She took his hand and they walked back to the dining room. Their food had just come out of the kitchen and the waiter was busy setting everything up.

"Looks delicious," she said.

"It is," he responded and reached out and squeezed her hand. "Thank you for tonight. I would have been sitting here all alone, wishing I had a good-looking woman to talk to me. I'm really enjoying being with you."

A smile spread across her face. "Thanks for asking me. I didn't realize how lonely I was until you asked me to dinner. This has been really nice."

For the next thirty minutes, they finished their dinner, laughing and talking and getting to know one another. Tanner was enthralled by this woman. If only he hadn't suffered that terrible time in Iraq, then he would not have this debilitating disease. Every day he prayed it would all just go away.

But it hadn't.

Finally, the waiter brought the bill. She opened her purse.

“No, this treat is on me. It’s been such a lovely evening and I would’ve had to eat alone if you had not joined me.”

“No, I want to pay my part,” she said.

“I insist,” he told her and quickly left the bills on the table. He stood and walked around and pulled out her chair.

“Thank you,” she said, “for dinner, the dancing, and just having fun tonight. This has been a real treat for me.”

Taking her by the elbow, they moved toward the elevators.

Would she turn him down? She didn’t seem like the type of girl who jumped into bed with just anyone, but then again, he didn’t believe in booty calls as such, and yet here he was begging God to please let him have tonight.

“Can I walk you to your room?”

“Yes,” she said, smiling. “I would like that very much.”

They walked onto the elevator. Going up, the machine jolted and made a popping noise and fear spiraled through him.

Please not now! Squeezing his eyes shut, he tried to think of what the therapist had told him. A pleasant memory, not of war, but of something he enjoyed.

With a deep breath, he relaxed when the door slid open and they stepped out toward her room. When they got to her door, she turned to him.

“I had a really great time tonight,” she said.

“Me too,” he said and his mouth came down on hers. Her eyes widened and then slid closed as he kissed her. As his lips moved over hers, it was all he could do to keep from begging her to let him sleep with her, for the two of them to spend the night in each other's arms.

She tasted of sweet ice tea and something else so refreshing that he pushed her against the door and pressed his body into hers, letting her feel his erection. Letting her know exactly how he felt about her. How much he wanted her.

It had been so damn long. And she was exactly what he wanted.

A moan escaped from her throat and he felt her fingers fumbling for the key lock.

Breaking the kiss, she opened the door and stared at him.

"Damn, it's been too long," she said as she pulled him into her room.

Joy overwhelmed him as he lifted her in his arms, his lips never leaving hers as he carried her to the bed.

"You're right," he said breaking the kiss. "Way too long."

CHAPTER 3

Early the next morning before the sun rose, Tanner woke and glanced at Emily as she lay on her side, curled away from him.

Last night had been incredible. All his fears of not being able to have sex again were now history. She had been so wonderful that he hated leaving her, but knew it was for the best.

A broken man like him didn't deserve a beautiful woman by his side like her. All she could ever be was a romantic rendezvous.

Carefully, he rose from the bed not to wake her and found his strewn clothes. They had been in such a hurry that they just tossed their clothes off and then fell into one another's arms. Never had he experienced such a wonderful time, but it couldn't last, and he'd lied to her from the get-go about who he was.

Women didn't like being lied to.

Gazing down at her, he loved her pert nose, full lips,

and high cheekbones where a piece of her blonde hair lay curled on her cheek. The urge to move it was strong, but he feared waking her.

They had made love until early this morning and she needed her rest.

Maybe he should leave her a note.

Finding a piece of paper in the dark, he quickly scribbled.

Have to go. Thank you for a wonderful night. Tanner

No phone number. No way for her to find him. And sadly that's the way it had to be.

There had been no promises made, except that they would enjoy each other, and that had been fulfilled many times over. No promises that this was more than a tryst.

Walking out of the door carrying his boots, he softly let the door click behind him.

It was all he could do to keep from dancing down the hall. He'd had sex. Great sex. And now it was time to go back home to his ordinary dull life.

Time to continue facing the disease he hated. Time for him to return to the family dude ranch where he and Travis dealt with the clients. Today, a new group would be arriving and the family would make certain they enjoyed their week.

With a grin, he got on the elevator and rode it up to his room on the top floor. There he showered, drank some coffee, and grabbed his things.

Time to go.

When he reached his truck, the sun was just beginning to rise and in two hours he'd be home. Back to his ordinary lonely life. Back to people walking around him staring at him strangely when he had an episode. Thank goodness, they didn't happen too often in public.

Once he was inside his truck, he called Tucker.

"Wake up, little brother," he said.

A sleepy, groggy Tucker answered the phone. "Do you know what time it is here? Someone had better be dead or you're going to be."

"No one's dead yet," he said.

"Did you pick up the new chef?"

"No, she decided to drive in, so I stopped last night at a hotel in Granbury."

"All right," Tucker said. "And that's why you're calling me before dawn."

"I did it," he said his voice so excited. "Last night I had the best damn sex of my life."

"With a prostitute?"

"Oh hell, no," Tanner said. "A beautiful woman I met at the hotel. At the swimming pool. She looks damn good in a bikini too."

There was a moment of silence on the phone. "No problems?"

"Not a one. My PTSD behaved itself and we did it three times last night. I couldn't get enough of her."

A chuckle came from his brother.

Pulling out onto the highway, Tanner knew he should hang up the phone, but he felt so excited about this trip that he just had to share it with his brother. Only he and Tucker knew how much he feared having sex again. It wasn't that he wasn't capable, but who wanted to sleep with a man who suddenly freaked out because he thought he was back in the war zone?

"Did you get her phone number?"

With a sigh, Tanner knew he should have probably asked for her number, but he just felt so uncertain about when an attack would suddenly happen. Last night, he'd slept like a baby and that had not happened to him in years. Normally, he had at least one episode a night.

Not last night. Last night, he'd slept so well beside Emily.

Oftentimes, a dream would take him back to Iraq, and then he would wake up fighting everything and anyone in the room. Twice he'd destroyed his cabin. Smashing glasses, tossing lamps, and even his TV.

"No, this was one night. One night only," he said. "You know I'm not capable of being with someone in a relationship."

Tucker made a noise on the phone. "If you found the right person, I think they could help you get over this."

There was little traffic on the freeway, but soon he would be turning off onto a winding highway. One where he would need to pay attention. One where he had to disconnect from his brother.

"But what if I hurt them? Sometimes, I wake up flailing my arms trying to fight off the demons in my dreams."

Sometimes he woke up, standing on the mattress ready to defeat the enemy, protecting his country, only to realize it was his cabin. No one knew how he'd destroyed his cabin. Not even the maids.

"That's what I mean," Tucker said. "This person could

help you come back and keep you from fighting in your dreams."

They could also run from him afraid of how he'd hurt them or almost hit them or something even worse. No, he could never have a permanent person in his life.

"No, I fear injuring someone. It's just better that I remain alone. At least until this goes away," he said.

If it ever went away. That was his biggest fear, that he would have to live this way for the rest of his life.

"But what if it never goes away?" Tucker asked. "If someone loves you, they can help you learn to live with this."

His brothers didn't understand what frightened him most was losing complete control, hurting the enemy only to wake up and realize it was the person he cared about the most. It was one reason he refused to stay at anyone's home.

There was no way he could endanger them. Not someone he loved.

"No, can't happen. Not until the doctor tells me this is gone and I'm okay," he said.

The doctor had not given him much hope for it ever disappearing.

"All right, but I wish you would at least try," Tucker said. "I'm happy for you. Now let me get back to sleep. I've got a wake-up call in two hours before I have to be on set with my new client."

"Who is it?"

"I'm not going to tell you," Tucker said. "But she's a

well-known artist who has the voice of an angel, the body of a goddess, and the strength of a lioness."

Though he could not have a lasting relationship with a woman, he wanted the best for his brothers. They both deserved happiness.

"Damn, you have all the luck," Tanner said. "Is she beautiful?"

"Gorgeous. But my job is to keep the idiots from coming after her. Some stupid asshole thinks she's supposed to marry him. And yes, she's so stinking beautiful, it's really hard."

Tanner laughed.

"Better you than me," Tanner said. "All right, I'll let you go. I'm getting off the freeway and onto the road to the ranch and you know how windy this stretch of highway can be."

"Congrats, Tanner," Tucker said. "But get over this being alone shit."

"Never," Tanner said as he disconnected. He wondered where his brother Travis was but knew better than to call. He and his new girlfriend were taking a week-long cruise together before she moved in with him at the ranch.

They had gone through a lot in the last month, and right now, they were having an unofficial honeymoon that he didn't want to interrupt.

Tanner was so happy for Travis and knew it had been a long rocky road for him and love. But at least now he had found someone he could spend forever with.

Turning on the radio, he listened to a country and western song and thought about Emily. He wondered what she thought this morning when she woke and found his note lying on the pillow beside her.

God, he wished he was there to kiss her good morning. To make love to her once again. To run his hands over her body and enjoy the sounds of her moans.

Time to return to the real world. Time to forget about his great night spent in the arms of a beautiful woman. Time to get back to the running of the Burnett ranch.

CHAPTER 4

Emily woke with the sun streaming through the hotel window and realized that Tanner was gone. With a sigh, she stretched and rolled over and smiled. Last night was the best night she'd had in over three years. Last night, she'd experienced one orgasm after another and could only thank the man who was no longer in her bed.

She rolled toward the pillow he'd been sleeping on and took a deep breath. It smelled of Tanner. The crunch of paper made her realize he'd left her a note.

Picking it up, she read the short and sweet missive. Oh, how she wished he'd left her his number. But that wasn't meant to be. Last night had only been about pleasure. Nothing else.

The experience had been for one night only. Both realized they were using each other and, oh, how they had used every inch of their bodies. But now it was over and it was a new day.

Time to move on to the next new experience in her new life.

Knowing she needed to get up and get going, she rose from bed. She had an hour before she needed to be on the road.

After she showered, she grabbed a bite to eat and a coffee to go. She needed to be at the ranch by noon. Her orientation would begin later this afternoon and they wanted to give her time to get settled in before she took over their kitchen tomorrow.

Cooking was her love and she couldn't wait to show them her talents. Talents she'd spent learning while John had been in Iraq.

While this job was on a smaller scale than the big restaurants in New York that had been recruiting her, she knew it would be less stressful and she needed peace. And she was looking forward to living in the middle of nowhere with the cows and an ever-changing guest list.

This seemed like the perfect opportunity to regain control of her life.

Away from the press and the constant reporters. Away from the town where everyone knew her story. Away from the sorrow that followed her like a shadow.

Last night only added to her peace. If she could tell Tanner thank you, she would. But he was gone. This morning she felt more relaxed and at ease than she had in years. No, she would never see him again, but she would always be grateful for the time they shared. For the pleasure-filled night that made her realize she could love again someday.

After loading her suitcases into her Volkswagen, she got behind the wheel. Next stop, her new job.

Putting the address in her phone, she followed the directions, enjoying the winding two-lane highway that led her deeper into Texas. Oak trees lined the road, the growth thick, making the drive a spectacular, beautiful view.

Two hours later, she saw the ornate gate and pulled into the Burnett Dude Ranch where she would be cooking.

Trees reaching to the sky lined the driveway. At the guard gate, she stopped. "I'm Emily Young, the new cook."

"Welcome, Mrs. Young. I'll tell the family you've arrived. Just pull up to the main building there and they will come and meet you. Good luck to you."

Pressing the gas, her Volkswagen bug tootled on down the road until she saw the main building where the kitchen resided, where she would spend her time doing what she loved.

Cooking.

Pulling into a parking place, she turned off the car and stepped out.

Several people hurried toward her.

"Hello," an older woman who walked with a cane said. "I'm Rose Burnett, the head of Burnett Enterprises. We met at your interview. Welcome."

Yes, Emily remembered the gray-haired woman who'd been large and in charge at the board meeting. With just a glance, she'd silenced several junior members.

"Great to be here," Emily said, glancing around at all the houses and the land. It was a huge ranch. She'd been here for a quick interview, but she'd been so nervous that day, she didn't remember much about the place. But now the memory of how much she'd enjoyed meeting these people returned.

The peace, the quiet, the solitude. It seemed like a truly magical place.

Just then a beautiful dark-haired woman came running up. "I'm Desiree Burnett. I handle the front office and also work with the maids. Welcome."

Like a butterfly, she flitted around.

"Thank you," she said. "I think we met at my original interview."

"Oh, yes," Desiree said. "Travis is not here right now. He's on a cruise and won't be back until tomorrow night. Tucker is in California on business."

"All right," Emily said.

Just then several other men walked up and she remembered their faces, but not their names.

"I'm Joshua Burnett and these are my brothers Jacob and Justin," the man said.

She remembered them from when she visited before. "Good to see you all again."

"There are a lot of us living here on the ranch. It's truly a family operation," Justin, the younger one, said.

Four more men walked up and she truly felt overwhelmed. "I'm James Burnett and these are my sons, Caleb, Cody, and Cameron. Welcome to the ranch."

"Thank you," she said, wondering how many more there were.

Then she saw him, and instantly she froze, her heart pounding in her chest.

Oh shit. Oh shit. Oh shit. What was he doing here?

With a gasp, she watched as Tanner strode up. His head tilted and he stared at her.

"Emily? What are you doing here? Why did you follow me?"

She swallowed and they were all gazing at them. What had she done?

"I didn't follow you. I work here. I'm the new cook," she said, wondering how this was going to go. What was he doing here?

Shaking his head, Tanner came right up to her. "You said your name was Emily Wilder."

"It is. Emily Wilder Young," she replied. "And you said your name was Tanner *Smith*. I gather that's not your *real name*?"

Snickers could be heard and she didn't dare look at anyone but Tanner. Staring into his emerald gaze, she could see the confusion there.

"No, it's Tanner Burnett. I didn't give you my real name."

A simmering anger sizzled through her as she stared at him. He lied. Lied to her about who he truly was. Could he also be married?

"You lied," she accused.

"You lied as well," he said.

"No, Emily Wilder is my maiden name."

There were guffaws as people around them moved nervously.

Staring at him, his eyes were darting emerald dagger at her and his face was red and tight with rage.

Did he think she had done this on purpose? Did he think she would have slept with him if she'd known he was part of the family she was going to work for?

All he had to do was be truthful and he'd failed at being honest with her.

Crap! She'd had sex last night with one of the owners of the ranch. Not good. Not good at all to learn on your first day on the job.

"I think you should leave," he said.

No, he was not going to bully her into leaving.

"Unless I'm fired, I'm staying," she said. "I'm the new cook. Why does it bother you that I'm here? Are you afraid I'm going to harass you? Believe me, I'm not."

He glared at her and she could see he wanted to say more, but what could he say that wouldn't embarrass them both? What could he say without confessing they had slept together last night?

"You know why," he retorted.

"It didn't seem to bother you last night," Emily said, returning his glares with her own. It had been a one-night stand. That's all and she accepted that's all it meant to either of them.

"It's over," she said with finality. "Get over it."

There were snickers in the background and Tanner's face turned red. She'd embarrassed him, but he would not seem to let go of the fact that he wanted her to leave. And she wasn't going anywhere. Not unless they fired her.

She glanced at Rose, who immediately understood.

"Come, Emily, and let's get you settled in. We'll fill out the necessary paperwork and get you a place to stay. Then later this afternoon, Desiree will give you a tour since Tanner seems to be inconvenienced by you being here. Why is that, Tanner? Do you have something to hide?"

It was all she could do not to laugh.

Inconvenienced my ass. It was just he hadn't expected her to show up at his ranch, and now, he was having to deal with the shock that he'd been caught in a lie and they had slept together.

"Nothing to hide. And no, Desiree taking over is not a problem," he said, his face turning red.

Liar.

"Tanner, my office, four p.m.," Rose said as she shuffled toward the main building.

With one last glare directed at the man she'd spent the night with, Emily walked away from Tanner and followed Rose. Oh my, how was this going to affect her being at the ranch?

Would they fire her if they learned she had slept with Tanner? It was obvious something had happened between them since they'd each given the other a different name.

"Don't know what happened between you and Tanner, but it's none of my business. All that matters is you do a good job cooking for our guests," Rose said.

"Thank you, ma'am. Tanner's issues won't interfere with my job, I promise you," she said.

But would it? Already she could tell he was angry. Why? It had been a single-night affair. Nothing more. She understood that and knew she would never see him again. What more did he expect?

She could handle the situation, but could he?

All he had to do was say *hello, Emily* and everything would have been fine. But no, instead, he'd made a scene and now everyone was guessing how they knew each other.

Not a good way to start a new job – sleeping with the boss.

CHAPTER 5

Tanner felt like he had been summoned to the principal's office for some grave misdoing. But he'd done nothing wrong, and he wasn't about to confess to his aunt he had spent the night in Emily's arms.

And what a night it had been. One he didn't regret but worried it would interfere now that he knew she was the new cook. It had been a one nighter, nothing more, nothing less.

One night of extreme pleasure spent in Emily's arms that he'd never forget.

"Explain to me why you treated our new employee so rudely. What has she done that you feel the need to tell her to leave?" his aunt said, gazing at him behind her large desk. "I've worked very hard to find a chef of her caliber to come to the ranch."

As the head of Burnett Enterprises, she wielded her power accordingly. She was the boss and he'd managed to trespass into her territory. He'd stepped on her toes and she wasn't taking his remarks kindly.

What could he say? From the way Aunt Rose was staring at him, he had to start talking and maybe he'd wanted to keep it private about what happened last night, but that wasn't looking possible. It seemed everyone would soon know where he'd been and what he'd been doing.

"I met her at the hotel last night," he admitted. "We had dinner."

She gazed at him. "You slept with her didn't you?"

He squirmed in his seat like he was nine not twenty-eight going on ninety.

"It was a night of mutual pleasure," he finally admitted.

That wasn't a lie. In fact, it didn't explain how wonderful the night had been. But at least it skirted the edges from the most passionate night he'd ever experienced.

"Did you tell her it was a one-night hookup? Did you lie to her?"

With his foot, he tapped the rug, not able to sit still. "No. I did lie about my name because I didn't want her to trace me back to the ranch."

Neither one of them had acknowledged that it was going to be just one night, but he assumed they both knew it could not last longer. She was traveling and he was only there for that night before he returned home.

His aunt shook her head and sighed. "How did that work out for you?"

"Obviously, not well. Just fire her, Aunt Rose. We'll find another chef."

The woman leaned over the desk. "Do you know how long it took me to find a good cook? She's a graduate of Escoffier School of Culinary Arts and earned the student chef of the year award from the American Culinary Federation. And you want me to send her packing? Are you crazy?"

Oh, she was not happy. Not happy with him at all.

"There's a better chance of me sending you packing. Keep your dick in your pants and leave my cook alone. Do you understand me?"

Stunned that his aunt had used the word *dick,* he knew he was in trouble.

"If this had been Joshua, I would not be shocked, but you? Do you realize she could sue us for sexual harassment? That you have made us very vulnerable to a lawsuit? The sad thing is I want to keep her. She's what we've needed and you screwed it up."

Never before had his aunt been so strict and stern with him. Her voice had risen to where she was one octave below yelling at him.

"Keep away from her, do you understand me? If I hear of you giving her any trouble or see you near her skirts, you'll be kicked off the property."

Wow, that was about the harshest punishment you could get from Aunt Rose.

All because he had experienced one night with the new girl. The first time he'd had sex in over five long years. One act between the sheets and he was being threatened with banishment. It just didn't seem fair, and yet if he argued, he'd find himself outside the parameters of the Burnett Ranch.

"Yes, ma'am," he said. "I didn't know who she was."

"And she obviously didn't know who you were or this would never have happened. But I'm not willing to start searching for a new cook because you could not keep it in your pants."

Travis needed to get back here quickly or Tanner would soon be looking for new employment.

"Now get out of here. I have work to do. And again, don't let me see you hanging around her."

Rising from the chair, he hurried out of his aunt Rose's office. Jumping on the elevator, he descended until it landed on the main floor. With a sigh, he pushed open the outside doors and bumped into Joshua.

His cousin grinned at him. "Did you get in trouble?"

"Yes," he said.

"You should have waited until the two of you were alone," Joshua said, standing outside the administration building. "Why did you confront her in front of everyone? We were all shocked."

He shrugged. "I was surprised to see her. It just came out."

"That's not how you handle a beautiful woman after having sex with her," Joshua told him.

He was known for being the family hound dog who got into more trouble with women. Already he'd had two false paternity suits filed against him. Thank goodness, he'd proved the babies weren't his.

A sultry summer breeze blew and Tanner ached with

the knowledge that Joshua was right, but this was his first fling and he was learning. Even so, that didn't mean he wanted her to stay. If she stayed, he feared what would happen between them. The chemistry had been off the charts explosive last night.

"She wasn't supposed to be our cook. When I met her, she didn't mention being a cook."

Thinking back, he realized she had said very little about her life. They had mostly talked about him working as a horse wrangler. In fact, he knew she was from Boulder and that she was previously married, but nothing more. Nothing.

Joshua laughed. "Sounds to me like neither one of you were completely honest with the other. Why didn't you tell her you were Tanner Burnett? Last night would never have happened if you'd been honest."

With a sigh, his mistake seemed to fill him with disgust. "Because I was trying to protect the family name."

"That's smart," Joshua said. "It's just your timing really sucked."

Too many people knew them in this area and he didn't want her to realize that his family owned a huge ranch and had billions between them. She wouldn't be the first gold digger to come looking for love.

"You had a hookup with a woman. I'm proud of you," Joshua said with a grin.

"It was the first time since I left for Iraq. It's the only way I'm ever going to be with a woman unless I hire one and I refuse to stoop that low."

"Well, now, you're going to have to face the consequences."

"Besides how do you know I slept with her?"

"It's obvious. Both of you were shocked at seeing the other one, and from the look on her face after you spoke to her, and your look. It was one of those *damn, I want you, but I can't have you* and *what the hell are you doing here?* kind of looks."

His cousin had just described how he'd felt when he saw her. If he could have, he would have taken her to his cabin and had his way with her once again. But not with the family gathered around.

And now not ever unless he wanted to be fired.

Sometimes his cousin was too smart for his own good. Sometimes it was hell working with your family and them knowing everything about you.

"Look, you've got some issues, but you've come so far since you came home. You're starting to crawl out of your shell and the old Tanner is peeking through all the armor you ply yourself with. Maybe she would be a good one to try to test a relationship with."

Oh no, that could never happen. He'd already done too much damage.

"Do you want to get me fired? Aunt Rose has forbidden me from getting anywhere near Emily."

Joshua laughed. "And you've let that stop you in the past? I know she's told us no before, but who has she sent packing?"

"No one, but I don't want to be the first."

"Tread lightly for a few days and then go at her again," Joshua said. "If anyone deserves a woman, it's you."

"Thanks, Joshua, you tell my cousins I said to stay the hell away from her."

Joshua laughed and walked on inside.

The next few days, he would be determining how he could convince her to pack her things and head back to where she came from. That woman was a temptation he didn't need.

CHAPTER 6

Tanner paced his small cabin, walking between the couch all the way to the kitchen, before he turned and walked back to the bedroom. At a little over twenty feet, it wasn't much bigger than the cabins they rented.

But it was his safe space. His place where he knew the only person he could endanger was himself. His home where he could face his demons alone.

And now he had to see Emily every day. Every day, he would have to look into those twinkling sapphire eyes of hers, see her long blonde hair and that cute little upturned nose and high cheekbones.

And worry that one of his hound dog cousins would try to take his place.

How in the hell had he managed to have an affair with the woman who was their new cook? Of all people for him to choose, it had to be her. And damn, but she was a temptation. Even today, he felt drawn to her like he wanted to touch her again. But that wasn't possible unless he wanted to lose his job.

When she interviewed the first time, he was in Dallas at the VA Hospital and had not met her. So he had no idea who she was and what she looked like. He had no idea he was playing with fire and about to get scorched – black-earth scorched if he wasn't careful.

How could he gaze at her every day and keep from touching her? He couldn't. All that sweet flesh of hers beneath her clothes. All that tempting softness and sweet-smelling woman would be way more than he could resist.

She couldn't stay. She had to go and he'd do everything he could to make certain she was out of here and soon.

Like tomorrow. Aunt Rose be damned. Emily had to leave.

It wasn't that he didn't enjoy last night, it was actually the opposite. There was no way he could continue to be around her without wanting more of her and that was impossible.

The sex had been incredible, but he could never have a permanent relationship. Last night was only supposed to be a single encounter. That's all.

Pacing the floor of his cabin, he tried to think of some way to convince her to leave. But, obviously, she must need the job for her to be working here.

"Why here? Why not some hifalutin restaurant in the big city? What had drawn her to the Burnett Ranch?"

As he asked the questions out loud, the smell of lavender filled the room and he stopped. The only smell associated with his PTSD was gunpowder, blood, and the smell of death – a stench he would never forget.

With a sigh, he knew what he had conjured. A ghost.

"I don't believe in you," he said. "I'm going to take my anxiety medicine if you appear. You are a hallucination. Get out of my head. Leave me alone."

"Tanner," the older woman's voice called out while she slowly appeared dressed just like she would have in the late eighteen hundreds in a long dress with a full skirt and apron.

"No," he said, turning away from her and heading to the bathroom to take one of his pills. This wasn't real.

"What's troubling you?" she asked in a sympathetic voice. "You seem upset."

Ignoring the apparition, he flipped on the bathroom light to search for his anxiety pills.

They were gone.

"Crap," he said, searching about wildly, wondering if one of the maids had taken them. "Where are my pills?"

He heard the bottle rattle and he whirled around.

"These pills?" the shimmering apparition said. "You don't need them. You're fine."

What did she know? He wasn't fine. There was a ghost rumbling around in his head and he kept seeing her.

"The hell I am. Give those back to me. I need them because of you," he said.

"Me? What have I done?" the older woman said.

Had he seen her in Iraq? No, the women over there wore hijabs and she didn't have one of those on. This was so strange to have a woman appear in his hallucinations.

This had only happened twice. Once before when he was leaving for the VA Hospital in Dallas and now.

All he wanted was for her to disappear. Get out of his vision.

"I don't believe in you. Give me back my pills, so I can make you go away," he said, reaching for them. His hand went right through her, but the bottle of pills she pulled away from him.

"Ayyy..." he yelled, realizing he'd "touched" her. She really was a ghost.

"Well, I believe in you, and this little bottle of pills only makes you groggy and tired. I can't have you walking around like some ghosts I know. Dead."

He couldn't believe the words he was hearing. In the morning, he would call the VA. He'd gone off the deep end. Having sex with Emily had driven him right over the edge into LaLa Land. Only he wasn't singing and dancing. He was staring at an old woman in a dress that he'd only seen in museums.

No, she wasn't real. Squeezing his eyes shut, he prayed that she'd be gone when he opened them.

Nope, she was still hovering right in front of him.

"Give me my pills," he said quietly, his voice low, his breathing heavy. "And then go away."

The woman shook her head. "We have much to discuss and plan. There is a certain new arrival that I heard you know. How do you know her, Tanner?"

Turning his back on the apparition, he tried to force her from his mind.

"I think she's the one for you. When she arrived, I saw

how at first you were excited and then you grew worried. You tried to run her off, but she stood up to you. That's the kind of woman you need. One to not be bullied by you."

Maybe he should just check himself into a hospital. Right now, he was certain he was certifiable crazy. That the war, the PTSD, and the hallucinations were returning and it must have all been driven by the sex he'd experienced this weekend. And then seeing Emily walking among his family.

So much had happened in the last twenty-four hours. Everything from the best sex of his life to his aunt reprimanding him, and now this apparition taking over his mind.

"You are not real. It's all in my mind," he said and he walked away from the smell of lavender.

Before, when he hallucinated, it was battle scenes. Places where he thought he was going to die. Places he returned to with the war raging around him, his buddies fighting beside him as they tried to stay alive. And so many of them perished. It was reliving the people he cared about dying and him fearing his own death.

Was this hallucination to let him know he would soon be dying?

Like a good soldier, he marched through the house, his feet in rhythm as he went to the door. Maybe the hot summer air would shake him out of this episode. But normally, he didn't know when he was in a hallucination.

Normally, he was in the episode, fighting. It wasn't until later that he realized he was here at home and that everything had been a lie.

"You can run out the door, but I'll follow you. You're next, Tanner," the voice said. "And I'm not going away. We should talk about how you are going to court Emily," she said.

"What? I can't go near her, and right now, she's very angry with me. I doubt she would ever want me back."

"We'll make it happen."

The woman was in his head, talking to him like they were friends. This was the strangest hallucination he'd ever experienced.

Opening the door, he glanced back and saw the woman hovering above his couch. "You're not real. Now put down my pills, so that when I return I can find them. They will make you go away."

She threw the bottle at him, and when they hit him on the chest, they fell to the floor, the lid came off and the precious anti-depressants scattered across the floor.

"I'll come back tomorrow and we'll discuss how you're going to court her," she said and suddenly disappeared.

Court her? His hallucination thought he was going to pursue Emily. Now he knew for certain that none of this was real. Because he knew he could never have a relationship with any woman. But especially not Emily.

Suddenly he realized it was silent in his cabin and he glanced around. The hallucination was over. Leaning down, he picked up the pills and put them back in the bottle. No, he didn't believe in ghosts.

Picking up a pill, he popped it in his mouth. He needed the soothing effects so he wouldn't experience any more crazy shit tonight. The PTSD hallucinations were bad, but this had been over the top.

If ghosts were real, he would have seen a lot of them in Iraq. Dead soldiers. Men he fought beside.

All of this happened because of Emily. They had that incredible night of experiencing pleasure and now his PTSD was off the charts. Just seeing her again this afternoon had caused it to act up once again.

This was all her fault.

Tomorrow, he would find her. Tomorrow, he would offer her a large sum of money to move on. He would help her pack her bags and leave.

Tomorrow afternoon, her little yellow bug would be sputtering up the drive and she would be gone. And he would stand there in the drive and wave bye-bye because he was a damaged man who could not ever have a long-lasting relationship with a woman. Even someone as beautiful and tempting as Emily.

CHAPTER 7

Emily hummed and did a little dance in the new kitchen she worked in. This evening would be her first meal and she had chosen bacon-wrapped pork loin with a maple syrup glaze, sweet potatoes, and asparagus for tonight's main course with apple crisp and ice cream for dessert.

This morning, she'd gotten online and ordered the food she would need for the next week and finished planning the meals for the next seven days. Everything was organized and she had her menus sent up to Aunt Rose for her approval.

The woman had been ecstatic at the way she had mapped out what they were having.

Desiree had promised to help her serve this evening, and so far, she felt in charge. After attending Escoffier School of Culinary Arts and winning the chef of the year award from the American Culinary Federation, she was confident in her skills as a chef.

The apple crisp was baking. The pork loins were ready to cook and the sweet potatoes were prepped and ready to go. Ahead of schedule, she was already looking at what she needed to prep for tomorrow morning's breakfast. Two bacon quiches were in the refrigerator ready to bake. One with peppers and one without. Except for a side dish of fruit, breakfast was prepped.

Looking through her cookbook, she hummed a song and shook her hips. This was her favorite place to be. This was where she found her joy.

"Excuse me," a deep voice said and she knew immediately who was in her kitchen.

Without turning, she continued to look at the different dishes she had planned for this week. "How can I help you, Tanner? Are you hungry? I think there is some leftover fruit from breakfast this morning."

She was not going to give him the satisfaction of letting him upset her. She refused to react to his nonsense. He'd ruined the best night of her life and she was still a little angry at him for causing so much trouble yesterday.

"Can we please talk?"

"About what?" she said, whirling around. "Nothing left to say. And I'm working right now."

He ignored her.

"About how you can't stay here," he said.

A smile crossed her face. "If you're afraid I'm going to go chasing after you and telling everyone what we did the night before last, you're wrong. We used each other. Unless you make a big deal, it's over."

She could see that her words stunned him and that's

exactly what she wanted. She didn't want him to know how hurt she'd been by his actions last evening. He had ruined a perfectly beautiful experience for her. He had soured her first time with a man since her husband.

It would have been fine if he'd said *hello, good to see you again,* but instead he demanded that she leave. He'd embarrassed both of them in front of his family. He practically admitted to what they had done, and yet, he still wanted her to leave.

"It was a one-night stand. Now, if you'll excuse me, I have a job to do."

With a smile, she turned back to the cookbook, ignoring him.

"I can't have you here," he said.

Turning back, she gazed at him. "Why not? Do you think I'm going to jump your bones at the first opportunity and then sue you for sexual harassment?"

What was the big deal about her working here? All they had to do was avoid one another.

"No," he said. "It's complicated, you have to go."

Suddenly she understood, and she was glad the kitchen knives had been put away. "You son of a bitch. You're married."

"No," he said, growing agitated. "I didn't lie. I've never been married."

"Then why do you want me to leave? I'm not going to pursue you. It was one night and if I'd known you were a Burnett, I would never have slept with you. I want and need this job."

She had walked away from everything in Boulder to

come here, and if he thought she would just pack up and go, he was sadly mistaken. She was not leaving.

Taking a deep breath, she tried to calm and lower the irritation in her voice. She was not going to cause trouble. She'd promised Rose that the fling with Tanner meant nothing.

Sadly, it was the first time since John that she'd been interested in a man, but after yesterday and today, it was just a memory of a good time that was tainted because of his bad manners.

"You can't be here. I can't have you around me," he said.

"Why? Are you a vampire and you're going to change me if don't leave?" She gave a little laugh. "Now that sounds interesting. A blood-sucking vampire who wants me to become one of his brides."

She gave a toss of her long blonde hair and turned back to the cookbook, hoping he would go away. Maybe if she ignored him, he would depart.

Glancing around the kitchen, she didn't want to leave. This was a dream kitchen setup and she could just imagine all the lovely dishes she was going to make in here, without Tanner Burnett.

She heard his footsteps walking up behind her and she whirled around to face him again, wishing he would just leave her alone. He stood less than a foot away from her. Close enough she could smell his tantalizing man smell. She could feel the tension radiating from him.

And the urge to reach up, wrap her arms around his neck, and pull him to her, was strong. But that wasn't going to happen.

"Here," he said approaching her. "You can find another job and—"

The timer on the oven went off. She pushed past him and pulled the apple crisp out to check the crust.

Perfect.

The kitchen filled with the smell of cooked apples and cinnamon.

She put the second one in and set the timer again. Both of them would be finished in time for the dinner in two hours.

When turning back to him, he shoved a piece of paper in her hand.

"Please be gone by tomorrow morning," he said and walked away.

She gazed down at the paper. It was a check for five thousand dollars. Rage filled her as she thought of what she'd gone through to come here.

Oh, hell no.

Stomping after him, she followed him into the dining room, which was thankfully empty.

"No, I'm not leaving," she cried out.

He whirled back around to face her.

Staring at him, she crossed her arms across her chest. "Are you such a weakling that one night of sex is going to ruin a working relationship? Unless your aunt fires me, I'm not going anywhere. I'm perfectly fine working beside you, knowing that we made a mistake that night. Believe me, I'm never going to think about it again or mention it to anyone. How you decide to handle it is up to you."

He turned red as he glared at her. "I'm not a weakling."

"Then why am I, a small petite woman, causing you so much terror? I moved over twelve hundred miles for this job. All I want to do is cook. I don't give a damn about you and your penis. Just leave me alone and we'll get along just fine."

A door slammed somewhere.

"You can't be here," he said and she didn't understand why.

"Are you planning on murdering me?"

"No, it's just that I suffer from..."

"From what? One-night standitis? Fragile penis syndrome? Fear of women? Tell me what about me is so frightening and I'll be sure not to do it. But I'm not leaving."

With that, she tore up the check and threw it at him.

Just as she was turning to walk away, she heard him say, "I suffer from PTSD."

Turning, she sighed. "Well, suck it up, buttercup. So do a lot of people. So did my dead husband. At least you're still *alive*."

With a heavy heart, she returned to the kitchen. John's episodes had been horrible. And somehow, she'd had sex with a man who suffered from the same disease.

God, she hated war. She hated what it did to people. She hated how it ripped a hole in your soul and left you feeling empty. How it took the man you loved and left you hollow while the whole town celebrated his life.

And all she could do was wish he'd never gone back to that damn war.

The memory of standing over John's grave while the military did a twenty-one-gun salute wrenched her heart.

Taking a deep breath, she threw open the fridge, more determined than ever to make this a great meal. It could be her last one here at the ranch, but it would be a damn good one.

One that even Tanner would enjoy.

CHAPTER 8

Tanner watched the guests' and his family's reactions to the food served that night and knew he'd lost.

Emily was here to stay unless she did something really stupid. No one had wanted to hear his excuses that they needed to fire her. From what he'd heard from the diners, Emily was not going anywhere. Tanner was the one who needed to learn to deal with the fact that he slept with the cook.

Desiree walked up to him. "I don't know what's going on between you and Emily, but let me just tell you, she can cook. Our guests were raving about tonight's dinner."

Standing back, he watched as the staff cleared the tables. Tonight was the get-to-know-you dinner with dancing afterward. Even the family joined in. Normally, he went to his cabin.

"So are you going to tell me how you know her?"

"No," he said, thinking this was not something you

shared with your family. Already he feared it would be getting out. Too many people had figured out what happened.

"Okay, then let's play Jeopardy. I'll take old girlfriends for one hundred."

"I'm not answering," he said.

"How about military girlfriend for two hundred."

"Has anyone ever told you how irritating you can be?"

"Sure," she said. "But I don't pay them any attention. How about previous sex partner for five hundred?"

He turned and glared at her, trying to keep his face from changing expression. His cousin was not a dumb woman, by any means.

Her brows lifted and her mouth formed a perfect "oh" expression. "Double jeopardy!"

"Aren't you supposed to be starting the dance tonight since Travis is on his cruise?"

She ignored him and continued to blather on about Emily. He should have done what his cousin Joshua said and just waited until they were alone to confront Emily, but then he'd tried that today with no luck.

"If it makes you feel any better, I really like Emily. She's smart and cool and a really great cook," Desiree said. "Does she cook as good in bed?"

Closing his eyes, he shook his head. "I wouldn't know."

"Is she spicy and sweet and good enough to eat?"

"Desiree," he said exasperated. "In about five minutes, I'm going to walk out that door instead of helping you. Is that what you want?"

With a sigh, his cousin shook her head. She reached out

and touched his arm. Most of the time, he would jerk back, but today it didn't bother him and he wondered why.

"Oh, Tanner, Sunday when you returned, I saw glimpses of the old Tanner. The happy-go-lucky man who was easygoing and not so strained and afraid. And then Emily arrived and I could see the panic on your face. The war is over. Bring back my cousin."

If only he could. The war still raged in his mind, only it came back whenever he became stressed or filled with anxiety. He just wanted it to go away permanently. To never experience an episode of the war again.

Didn't she realize that he wanted to go back to being that fun guy who liked to laugh and tease and flirt? Somehow he'd lost himself in Iraq. Somehow he felt like that person no longer existed.

"Time to start the dancing," he said in response.

Desiree went out to the center of the floor. The tables were all neatly stacked in place, with chairs along the wall for people to sit and watch.

Travis always did this and this was Desiree's first time.

"Welcome, everyone," Desiree said, "we're so glad you're here. And wasn't that an excellent dinner tonight from our new chef Emily Young? We're so excited to have her on board with us. We've got a fun-filled week planned for all of you. But tonight is about getting to know everyone and a dance party. My cousin Cody is our DJ. Put in your requests with him. So dust off your dance slippers and let's have fun tonight. First up is the chicken dance."

She grabbed his hand and pulled Tanner out to do the polka with her. Just what he didn't want to do, but as soon as he could, he'd be walking out the door and going to his cabin.

When the song ended, they walked off the floor together.

"You know, I've been thinking. Maybe you should be nice to Emily. If I recall, she had a husband in the military who didn't come home."

Tanner glanced at Desiree. That was what Emily had been referring to earlier today. Just then she came out of the kitchen. He could see from her eyes that she was tired and probably wanted to go home.

Part of him said he should apologize while the other part screamed no. He didn't want her here. And yet he knew that was a lie as well. If she stayed, he was certain to take advantage of that sweet mouth of hers again.

"Let me worry about my relationship with Emily," he told her. "You take care of our guests."

"Oh no, I'm going to worry about you as well," she said. "Frankly, I'm hoping this girl will wake up the good man inside you. I know he's in there somewhere. He needs a good woman to show him that life is for the living and he's still alive."

"I left that man behind in Iraq," Tanner said. "His body is strewn on a minefield."

"Not funny," Desiree said. "Don't you think I worried every day that would happen to you? Don't you think we said a prayer every night for your safekeeping? Not funny at all."

With a whirl, she turned and walked away from him.

Great, he'd pissed off another woman. He was really good at making women mad.

Tanner liked keeping his family at bay. This way he didn't have to explain the scars on his soul. Battle did strange things to a person. Especially when you saw someone you cared about blown up or shot in the leg and then the Taliban finish them off before you could reach them.

War was like dying a little each day, only you were still breathing.

The only way he'd ever return to the desert would be on a suicide mission. And he would take out as many of the enemy as he could before he died.

"Excuse me," that sweet voice he enjoyed said, bringing him back to the present. "You're the only Burnett around and I need someone to lock the freezer for me."

Glancing down at the petite woman who could still make his heart flitter and his dick get hard, stared up at him. Those sapphire eyes and full sweet lips were a temptation he found hard to resist.

Right now, he just wanted to pick her up and carry her out the door to his cabin. He wanted to go all caveman and keep her in his bed for a week.

"I wouldn't bother you, but I can't find anyone else and I'm done for the evening."

It was a rule that the kitchen and freezer were to be locked when the cook left for the night. Mainly to keep inquisitive guests from getting into trouble. Nothing like opening up the kitchen in the morning to discover it had been raided by a guest.

"I've got a key," he said. "I'll take care of it later."

"No," she said, shaking her head, her eyes firm. "I need to see you lock it up. I'm not leaving before you do. Don't want to get fired for trusting the person who would love to see me terminated."

One thing he could definitely say was that the woman had spunk. And he couldn't blame her for not trusting him. He'd done everything possible to get her to quit.

"All right, let's lock everything up," he said. "Do you want a witness?"

"No, it would be your word against mine, and frankly, everyone knows you want to get rid of me, so I'd have a strong case."

They walked into the kitchen and the urge to apologize to her was strong. He'd been wrong, but he just wasn't ready to admit to her that she was right. Not yet. Not until he was certain his plan of urging her to leave would not work.

That was probably wrong, too, but right now, he was just trying to adjust to her being here and everyone disagreeing with him that she should leave.

Taking out his keys, he locked the freezer, and then they walked out the door of the kitchen and locked it behind him.

"Satisfied?"

"Yes, thank you," she said. "Now I'm going to my cabin."

"Can I walk you there?"

Why he offered, he didn't know. But it just sprang from his lips and he wanted to see her safely home.

"No," she said. "I don't want to be accused of coming onto you. I'm avoiding you if you haven't noticed."

Unfortunately, he had.

"I just wanted to make certain you got to your cabin without stepping on a rattlesnake or a coyote trying to eat you."

She raised her brows in disbelief. "The only coyote or snake I'm afraid of is standing right in front of me."

He grimaced. "Cute."

He'd deserved that and he couldn't blame her.

"Besides, that walk is my time to glance at the stars and just enjoy the peaceful night sky. I don't need any trouble. I don't need any frustration. It's a quiet time to reflect."

She turned to leave and he called, "Watch out for the vampires."

"Suck it," she said.

And he couldn't help but laugh. The woman had an attitude and unfortunately, he liked it. Unfortunately, he liked it way too much and it was going to be hard to resist.

CHAPTER 9

Emily walked into her cabin and glanced around at her lodgings. It was small, but neat and trim, and she had a place for all her belongings that she'd brought with her. Of course, not much fit in a Volkswagen Bug.

Most of her stuff she'd sold before she slipped out of town, not telling anyone her destination. Needing to be away from all the sadness.

But now she was here in Texas and adjusting to her new life.

The last two days had been tense with starting a new job, Tanner wanting her fired, and the feeling of sadness that suddenly overcame her. That night had obviously meant nothing to him, and while she had known what she was doing, she still wanted the act of the two of them joining to have meant something.

Not hearts and flowers and forever after, but about new beginnings.

For her, it was a step toward a new life and putting the past behind her.

For him, it didn't mean a damn thing, except that he wanted her gone from the ranch. And he'd lied. That was a hard one to understand, but then again, if he'd said Tanner Burnett, she would never have slept with him.

If only he'd been honest.

Slipping off her shoes, she slowly removed her chef's coat and put it on the stack of dirty clothes.

Her first day off was next week, and by then, she would have to search out a laundry facility.

Going into the small bedroom, she sank down onto the bed and leaned back. Maybe a quick shower before she crawled under the sheets and maybe read one of John's letters. No, she wasn't doing that any longer.

Before, she would read his letters to try to stay close to him. But it was time to put all that away.

She'd read a book or watch the news. Anything to keep from thinking about John or even Tanner. Time to concentrate on finding a new dessert or even a new main dish. She'd peruse her cookbooks until she grew sleepy.

Jumping up, she went into the bathroom and hopped into the shower. Ten minutes later, she came out and crawled into the bed.

The smell of lavender filled the room and she wondered where it was coming from.

Suddenly, a shimmering old woman stood before her, wearing a dress from the late 1800s with a white apron covering the full skirt. She hadn't seen a dress like that except in museums.

"Hello," she said. "I hope I don't frighten you."

Speechless, Emily didn't move. This job had sent her over the edge. The moving, Tanner, and dealing with everything had finally caught up with her. She'd gone crazy and was now seeing ghosts.

A tingle of fear spiraled up her spine. Why was she here?

"I'm Eugenia Burnett," she said. "Yes, I've been dead for a long time, but I still worry about my family."

Dear God, this was the woman who helped start this ranch. Was she real or was Emily crazy? Did she realize her family was doing very well?

"I'm worried about Tanner," she said.

No, she couldn't be here to talk about Tanner. Oh no. Not going to happen.

"Someone told me that your husband was in the military," she said. "Is that true?"

No, she wasn't talking to a ghost about her dead husband either.

"What do you want?" Emily asked bluntly. This was all so weird.

"I want my grandchildren to be happy. To find someone to love, get married, and have babies. This family must continue on."

Now that was funny. How many single Burnett men had she met that first day? All of them good-looking, rich cowboys who wore tight jeans and western shirts with cowboy boots that cost more than her salary.

"There are enough Burnetts running the ranch that I don't think you're going to have a problem," Emily said, thinking most of them probably had a girlfriend. Someone since they were so handsome. "I think you'll soon be able to start your own country, there are so many of them."

"Yes, but how many of them are married? None. Even Travis has not married the girl I introduced him to."

That was weird. How did a ghost introduce two people? *Oh, hi, I'm your dead grandmother and I'd like to introduce the two of you*. If that didn't send a girl running from a man, she didn't know what would.

"Sounds like a problem," Emily said. But it wasn't her problem.

The ghost gave a smile. "I knew you would understand. I like the way you stand up to Tanner. That's what that boy needs. A strong woman who will not take crap from him, as you young people like to say."

Oh no, she was not going to try to set her up with Tanner. That was not going to happen.

"Why are you talking to me about Tanner? I'm sure you've heard that we're not exactly friends."

The ghost gave a little laugh. "But you could be."

Oh no, she didn't know what this ghost was up to, but for one, she didn't really believe in paranormal sightings, and two, she would never let a ghost hook her up with Tanner.

"I'm a widow. A recent widow like three years ago. My husband was in the military; he had PTSD and I'm not going to accept another man with that issue. Been there, done that, and got the damn visit from the military saying *we regret to inform you...*"

The memory of those two officers showing up at her

doorstep was like a slap to the head. Especially with the news they delivered.

The ghost seemed to try to touch her and Emily backed against the headboard.

"Oh, sweetie, I was a widow twice and it's the worst. I'm so sorry about your husband. It's just my boy needs some love and understanding, and I think you're the perfect person to help him."

Oh, if this ghost only knew what had gone on between the two of them. She would be long gone. A spontaneous meeting in a hotel was not exactly the kind of action a grandmother would approve of for her grandson.

"No, not going to happen. Tanner wants me fired. He'd gladly walk me out of here tomorrow if he could."

"That's because he's afraid of the feelings he has for you," the woman said.

Emily was insane. She was lying in bed, talking to a ghost who wanted her to help Tanner. What was wrong with her? And the dead woman was saying that Tanner had feelings for Emily.

Bad feelings.

"The only feelings he has for me is he's sorry, he—" The words just seemed to slip from her mouth. She wasn't about to tell this older woman, a ghost, that she'd slept with her grandson. Of course, that might send the specter running or it might bring trouble. And tonight, she just wanted to rest.

"Look, you need to go. It's been a long hectic day, and tomorrow, I have to serve breakfast at seven a.m. which means I have to start cooking at six. I need my beauty rest."

The ghost gave a little laugh. "You definitely are a blunt person. Exactly what Tanner needs."

"No," Emily said again. "Don't be thinking of ways to get us together. I'm avoiding him and he hates me. There is no way we'll ever get together. I'd suggest looking for another woman or starting on another of the Burnetts. As for me, I'm rolling over and going to sleep. If you want to stay, you can, but I'm going to sleep."

The idea of someone watching her sleep was creepy, but she hoped the unwelcomed visitor would get the hint and leave.

The ghost dissipated and disappeared. "I'm not giving up on you two."

"You must like to be frustrated," Emily said as she rolled over and closed her eyes.

Good grief, was she really talking to a ghost? What the hell was wrong with her? Had anyone else in this family experienced this? She mentioned that Travis had not married the woman she found for him.

"Good night, dear," the ghost said.

With a groan, Emily put the pillow over her head. She had to sleep and this was not helping.

CHAPTER 10

The next morning, Emily could not get the ghost visit out of her head. Had it been real or had she just gone into some kind of haze from being so tired and stressed? She didn't know, but she thought there might be one person who could tell her.

Desiree. The woman was her go-to for any questions she had about the ranch. After all, she was a Burnett and she knew so much about the family, the ranch, and everything going on here.

This morning's breakfast serving had been a huge hit with the guests and she had lunch already prepared. It would be a salad bar with their choice of taco meat or sliced turkey.

The salad bar was set up and she just had to put the vegetables out. The taco mixture was simmering and the lunch meat was chilling in the fridge.

Desiree entered the building and Emily waved at her.

"When you get a minute, I need to speak to you," she called.

The girl smiled, and Emily went back to fixing the strawberry cake she was preparing for tonight.

A few minutes later, she came into the kitchen.

"Oh, that looks delicious. I'm tempted to steal a piece right now."

"Don't you dare," Emily said with a laugh. "It's for tonight."

"I'll definitely be here. What's wrong?"

How did she tell her what had happened last night without sounding like a total nut job?

She poured the cake batter into the pan and slid it into the oven.

"After I got back to my cabin last night, when I crawled into bed, the strangest thing happened."

Desiree put her hand to her forehead and shook her head. Why did Emily get the feeling that she knew what she was going to say?

"A ghost appeared before me. She said her name was Eugenia Burnett. I don't believe in ghosts, and yet, she spoke to me."

A sigh escaped from Desiree. "That's my great-great-great-great-grandmother. She's come back and has been trying to matchmake us. She's worried the family line is going to die out."

"So I'm not crazy?"

"No," Desiree said with a laugh. "But I'm warning you, when you receive a visit from Eugenia, that means she has someone in mind for you, and she'll go to any lengths to put the two of you together."

Just what Emily did not need: a matchmaking ghost.

"I'm not interested and I told her that," she said.

"Doesn't matter. Who is she trying to match you with?"

"Tanner, and we all know how well that's going," Emily said.

Desiree busted out laughing. "The man doth protest too much."

"I'm just here to cook. Nothing else. Why he's so worried I'm going to jump his bones, I don't know, but he has nothing to worry about. And Eugenia is going to be very disappointed. It's not going to happen."

Just then, a group of guests came through the door. "Gotta run, it's arts and crafts time. We'll talk more later. But I'm warning you, she's a stubborn old woman who normally gets her way."

"Well, she hasn't had to deal with me."

Desiree laughed as she went out the door.

Maybe Emily should make a door hanger for Tanner. She could needlepoint the words *Stay out. Go away. Not interested.*

But as much as she wanted those words to be true, they weren't. And that hurt. That first night had been wonderful, fantastic, so many expletives, but it had not cured her of wanting Tanner. Only, now, she had to avoid him at all costs.

As she turned to go back into the kitchen, Tanner came through the door.

A groan escaped her lips and she hurried back inside her domain, hoping he wouldn't follow her.

"We need to talk," he said.

"I need to cook dinner," she replied.

"You said something about your husband the other day," he said, ignoring her.

"Yes," she replied as she went to check on her cake. It was just starting to brown. "What about him? He's dead."

If he thought she was going to tell him about John, he was definitely insane. She'd just run from a city that thought that they had to remind her every day of the sacrifice her husband made. While all along she knew the truth.

And it ate at her soul like a cancer.

"You told me at least I'm alive," Tanner said. "Did he die in the military?"

"I'm not going to talk about this, right now," she said. "I'm trying to cook dinner. I'm working and it's none of your business."

Tanner leaned against the counter. "I'm not going away until you tell me."

Stopping, she stared at him. "All right. I'll tell you about John if you'll tell me about your great-great-whatever-grandmother Eugenia."

His eyes popped wide as he leaned forward. "You saw her?"

"Yes, she came to visit me last night and all she wanted to talk about was you."

"No, I don't believe in her. It's my disease."

"Well, then I have it as well," Emily said. "Your disease is contagious. We have seeing-ghosts disease."

She could tell he didn't appreciate her humor.

"Not funny." Tanner shook his head and she could tell he was not happy. "Travis warned me."

"What did he warn you about?"

The man walked away from her, running his hand through his hair. Suddenly he no longer seemed interested in learning about her dead husband and that was perfectly acceptable to her. She didn't want to tell him about John. That was private and she'd escaped Colorado with the express purpose of putting her husband and his service behind her.

"Never mind," Tanner said, walking back to her, his eyes had darkened and he appeared angry.

Why wouldn't he tell her what Travis had warned him about? Did it have to do with the ghost?

"I'd like to know how I keep her from coming into my cabin," she said. "I wanted to go to bed and she wanted to talk about how I was perfect for you. Boy, she doesn't know how you feel about me, does she? You should tell her."

"How do I feel about you Emily?" he asked, moving closer.

Oh no, she didn't like that look in his eyes. There was passion there and they had no business exploring that particular feeling.

"You tell me. All I've heard lately is that you want me fired. You want me to leave. Pack my stuff and go back home. Let me tell you, I don't have a home anymore," she said, thinking of the cute little house she and John had purchased.

After three years of seeing him in every room, she'd sold it.

"That's because I can't have you here. You're a constant temptation. One I don't need," he said.

"Don't worry. Nothing is going to happen. Not even your grandmother is going to convince me that you're the man for me. She wants to continue the Burnett line. She wants her grandsons to marry and give her babies."

"I don't believe in ghosts," he said. "She's part of my hallucinations from the war."

Emily shook her head. "So I'm sharing your hallucinations? Think again."

"No, I don't believe in her. Someone has been filling your head with nonsense. Probably Desiree."

At first, he believed her and now she could see he was putting up walls, and she didn't appreciate him thinking she had lied to him about Eugenia. In fact, it just irritated the hell out of her.

"Get out of my kitchen and don't come back," she said, turning her back to him. "I know what I saw and Desiree had not said a word about her. She decided to come to my cabin and talk about you. A very sore subject."

"You were going to tell me about your husband," he said, stepping in front of her.

A laugh escaped her. Why in the hell did he think she would talk to him about her dead husband if he didn't believe her? That wasn't going to happen.

"Not after you think I lied about your grandmother. I've got work to do and no time to put up with your nonsense. Go talk to Desiree. Go talk to Travis about Eugenia. I'm going to hold a seance in my cabin tonight, and by golly when I'm done, she'll be gone."

A smile crept across his face. The first one since he'd walked in the door. Why did he think that was funny? Of all the things to find humor in, that was the last one she would have laughed at.

"Let me know how that goes for you," he said and walked out of the kitchen laughing.

Why was he laughing? She'd said it as a joke, but now, now she wanted to try her hand at seeing if she could get the woman to disappear. Why were seances funny?

CHAPTER 11

Tanner could not settle down tonight. As much as he wanted to go to sleep, he knew Emily was going to hold a seance at her cabin. When his great-great-great-great-grandmother was alive, she'd gone to several seances and that was how his great-great-great-great uncle had met his wife, Rose. The woman had been holding fake seances and taking people's money.

Until Uncle Travis put a stop to that and his mother, Eugenia, retaliated by moving Rose into their ranch home. The same house that his current living Aunt Rose lived in today. The same place the original family lived.

As much as he didn't want to believe, if that truly was Great-grandmother Eugenia, she would love the fact that Emily was holding a seance. She would delight in attending. There was no telling what she would do.

Glancing across the way at her cabin, he could see the lights were still on. It was getting late. What if she'd gotten hurt? Did ghosts hurt humans?

The tales of how Eugenia had been seeking information about his Great-great-great-great Uncle Tanner, who had been lost in the Civil War, returned and he knew he had to check on Emily.

He should have warned her. He should have told her his family history, and yet, he didn't want to admit that Eugenia was real. He didn't believe in ghosts. No matter what anyone said, he just couldn't accept she was a spirit coming back from over a hundred years ago.

How could he believe in ghosts when his mind kept returning him to the battlefield? Didn't he have enough problems?

Walking across the yard and the road, he went up the steps to Emily's cabin. He tried to glance inside but saw nothing.

Knocking on the door, he waited impatiently, shifting his weight from one foot to the other, worried about her. And until he knew she was safe, he couldn't sleep.

After glancing out the window, she opened the door in her pajamas.

Thank God, they were not of the sexy variety, but rather silk that clung to her every curve with yellow Volkswagens on them. Damn, he'd like to take a ride in her cars. Wherever they wanted to take him, he was willing to go.

"What are you doing here?"

"I was worried about you. Before I could go to sleep, I had to make certain you were all right."

"Why wouldn't I be fine?"

"Because you said you were going to hold a seance," he said.

She laughed and stepped out onto the porch in her pajamas. "We're having it now."

He tried to see around her to see who was inside, but she stood in the way. No noise came from inside.

"There's no one here, Tanner," she said. "I wouldn't know how to hold a seance and you need more than one person. I don't like to play with that supernatural-mojo stuff."

With a sigh, relief filled him. She was safe.

She sank onto one of the wooden steps and he sat beside her. A warm night breeze blew.

"Did Eugenia come tonight," he asked, still not certain he believed in the ghost, but so many people had seen her including him, if that was what she was.

"I've been alone all evening. Another five minutes and I would have been in bed," she said.

The memory of her firm curves snuggling up against him had his breathing accelerating. The thought of her in bed was not what he needed to think about. Even sitting beside her here in the darkness was dangerous. If his Aunt Rose caught them, he could be fired. And frankly, he didn't care.

"Did Desiree talk to you about Eugenia?"

"Yes, but after I saw her. What's the deal with the séance? From your expression, I knew there was something there."

For the next five minutes, he told her the family history that Eugenia went to seances trying to learn about her missing son, Tanner. The man he was named after. He recalled the tale of how Rose had a business pretending she could speak to the dead. Only, her sons, Travis and Tucker, the town marshal, didn't approve.

A giggle came from her. "Your family is very interesting. We don't have matchmaking ghosts in my family. We don't have a ranch over one hundred years old."

A piece of her blonde hair slipped from behind her ear onto her cheek and he pushed it back, wanting to see her face in the semi-darkness. The small porch light glowed behind them.

The way she stared at him made his heart pound. They were not fighting. No, tonight there was that connection they felt at the hotel, and that was dangerous. So dangerous to be here alone with her when all he wanted to do was carry her into her cabin and throw her on the bed.

"Tell me about your husband," he said, unable to resist. He had to know if she had experienced PTSD before.

With a sigh, she gazed out at the darkened road and the moon shining. It was such a perfect night and he had to resist the urge to pull her snug against his body. Cicadas chirped their lonely sound, searching for a mate.

"Why can't we just sit out here and enjoy the night breeze? Enjoy being with one another, looking at the stars."

It was strange that she would even want to spend time with him after the way he'd treated her these last few days.

"Because I don't know how to do that," he said quietly. "And regardless of how much I want to keep you away, I'm drawn to you. Those are the things that lovers do."

She turned and smiled at him. "Well, thank you. But you've made it clear you don't want to be with me. I just want to enjoy the evening breeze."

He deserved that. She'd been nothing but kind and he'd been trying to run her off the ranch. Even now, he believed she would be better off not here.

"Since you don't seem to want to talk about your husband, I'll be honest with you."

Her brows rose in the dark and she leaned her chin on her hand, her elbow braced on her knee as she turned and stared at him.

"I suffer from PTSD," he said.

"Yes, you told me." She responded like it didn't matter to her.

"And you told me that at least I was alive," he said.

"Yes," she replied. "John is dead and he had PTSD."

It was all he could do to keep from asking her how he died. Was it in battle or had he come home and succumbed to this disease and killed himself? So many soldiers died fighting the war inside their heads.

"For two years," Tanner continued, "I've battled this horrible sense of fear of returning to battle at any moment. It's not something you want to subject someone you care about. I'm doing much better, and even the doctor at the VA hospital keeps telling me that I may be one of the lucky ones who eventually puts this behind him. But until then, I can't be with a woman."

Even her. Especially her.

"Except for sex," she said. "That you're very capable of doing. It's the hard part – the being with someone on a regular day-to-day basis – that you fear."

He didn't even know what that was like. The only relationship he'd been in had been back in high school and that ended before he left for college.

"You were the first since I've returned," he said softly. "And it was special. But you're right. At any moment, something may send me hurtling back in time to a battlefield and I fear what I will do. What if I hurt you or a family member?"

She glanced at him and he could see her eyes were wide and innocent in the darkness.

"Maybe you should stop living in fear," she said. "It's why I moved to Texas. To start over. To begin again. You were my first since John," she said. "And I didn't expect anything more. But when you tried to have me removed from the new job I'd just driven over twelve hundred miles to reach, it kind of pissed me off."

A grin spread across his face. "Yeah, that would make me angry too."

"Why couldn't we be friends? I would never have made you feel like you had to date me or anything else when I arrived. I would have said 'Hello, Tanner. Good to see you' and walked on."

"But I couldn't," he said and instantly regretted it.

The woman just didn't get it. Even though she wanted to be friends, he wanted more than that, and if she was here, she would be too much of an enticement. Just like now, sitting out here in the dark in her pajamas with him, it was everything he could do not to kiss her.

And, God, he wanted to.

Oh, to hell with it. He was tired of fighting this attraction.

He grabbed her face and brought her lips to his. At first, she was pliant, her mouth conforming to his as his lips moved over hers. At first, she returned his kiss, her lips moving over his, her mouth opening to receive his tongue as he delved into her mouth, pulling her body close to his.

At first, she molded her body against his like she wanted him. But then, suddenly, she pushed him away.

"We can't," she gasped. "I like this job. I can't get involved with you."

Rising, she hurried into the cabin and closed the door behind her. He heard the lock click and knew she was done.

And still, she had not talked to him about her husband. What was she hiding?

CHAPTER 12

Emily locked the door behind her and tried to control her racing heart. If they had continued kissing, she feared she would soon be pulling him into her bed and that could not happen.

Even though her body responded to his kiss and her insides ached with the knowledge of what it would be like to have him deep inside her, she could not do it again.

As a new employee, she knew they could fire her in the first ninety days for no reason. And she liked this job. Even with Tanner being a pain in the ass, she enjoyed the people; she liked cooking for the guests, and she was excited to wake up each morning knowing her kitchen awaited her.

She didn't need Tanner to get her fired. Here on this ranch, she felt at peace, and it had been so long since she'd known that feeling. She didn't want it to end.

Climbing into bed, she turned out the light. The smell of lavender filled the room, and in the semi-darkness, she saw the ghost materialize.

No, not tonight. She'd dealt with enough for one day.

"I saw you kissing Tanner," Eugenia called. "Are you falling in love with him, dear?"

"No, I'm trying to sleep," Emily said, figuring it was impossible to relax when a dead person was speaking to her. It was kind of creepy. She didn't fear the ghost, but to think that a dead person was hovering around her room while she tried to sleep was chilling.

The woman laughed. "Oh, dear, you'll get plenty of time for that when you're dead."

Now, that was an unsettling reminder that she wouldn't live forever.

"Do you like my grandson?"

What could she say? Did the woman even know they had premarital sex? How would she feel about that? Emily was tempted to tell her, but then again, you didn't want to piss off a dead person. They could get even in ways she couldn't begin to imagine.

"Yes, Eugenia, I like Tanner. But there's a problem. If you truly want us together, then go visit him. He's the one who doesn't believe that he can be in a relationship with a woman. He's the one who isn't ready for a commitment."

There was silence, and for a moment, Emily thought the woman had left. But then she spoke. "What about you, dear? Are you ready to settle down forever with my grandson?"

"No, I'm not," Emily said, sitting up. "Since I'm not going to get any sleep, let's talk about my reasons why this is not a good thing."

Time to give up on sleep and deal with yet another problem.

Emily flipped on the light and sat up against the headboard. Eugenia sank her weightless body into the chair in the room.

"Tell me why not?" Eugenia said softly. "We'll fix this problem."

"It's not fixable," Emily said. "I'm a widow. Three years ago, my husband died in Iraq at the airport. He was helping refugees get on the plane when a bomb exploded killing him. His commander told me he threw himself over the bomber to save the women and children that were nearby. Damn him."

The ghost sat, astonished, not saying a word, while the tears that Emily hated slipped down her cheeks. Why did he have to die a hero? It was his last tour of duty and then they were going to open their own restaurant, start a family, and enjoy their lives.

After that tour, they would've had all the time in the world. Only problem was he came home in a box.

She knew how to live with his PTSD, but she didn't know how to live without him.

Damn him for dying and leaving her alone.

"I'm so sorry, dear, that your husband died a hero. All wars are bad and my idea of a great future was for there to be no more wars where men and women died. But don't you think your husband would want you to move on? You're young; you're beautiful. Don't you want a family of your own?"

What did this woman want from her? Blood? Because

she wanted her to remember a life path that suddenly had a roadblock thrown in.

"Yes, we were going to have children when he returned. But he never came home. He saved people's lives instead of coming home to me. Yes, I'm a selfish person. But I loved him. I wanted to spend my life with him."

Tears slipped down her cheeks and she knew she should have said this to Tanner tonight, but this was the reason she kept this information to herself. Even three years later, it was difficult.

It wasn't that her heart wasn't ready to fall in love again. She did indeed want a family and a man to cuddle beside her. And yet she was afraid. What if a new man pulled a selfless act and left her alone? What if this life path also had an impossible obstacle?

No matter how many times she told herself she was being selfish, that John had died a hero, it still hurt that he was gone and she was alone. In some ways, she almost felt angry that he had acted so heroically. And yet she knew that he was that kind of man. It was one of the reasons she'd fallen in love with him.

"Have you told Tanner this?"

"No," she responded. "Tonight, he asked me about John, but I try not to talk about him. His death is the reason I left Boulder. I'm trying so hard to start over without people knowing how John died a hero. To live my life to the fullest, but I'm not ready to love and marry again. Not even for Tanner."

Eugenia flew into the air and laughed. "Honey, I think you're more than ready. I've seen how it is between you and Tanner. You keep believing those lies you're telling yourself. But I think you're perfect for each other. You can help him with his PTSD — whatever that is. And he can help you see that your husband wants you to go on living without him."

Either Eugenia was as stubborn as Tanner or she didn't want to understand how Emily felt about her dead husband. Why couldn't people leave her alone and just let her cook? It was there she found comfort. It was there she felt happiest, in the kitchen.

The one-night stand they shared had been perfect for her. No commitments, just a night of joyous sex. But even that, Tanner had managed to ruin with him telling her to leave.

But the dude ranch was the place for her. She'd disappeared from the Boulder scene where the news organizations liked to constantly do stories on her and John. What a great man he was—how he left her all alone. Yada, yada, yada. Over and over, until she had wanted to run out of town screaming.

She yawned. "I've got to get some sleep. I have to work in the morning."

Eugenia chuckled. "I'll leave, but I think you and Tanner should at least go out on a date."

"We can't. Aunt Rose would fire him."

"Fiddle-dee-dee. No, she won't. Not unless she wants to have a lot of sleepless nights with me singing her to sleep."

Emily giggled at the thought of a ghost singing to show her displeasure. But it was also a reminder she could do the same to her. Maybe she should invest in a good set of earplugs. “Good night, Eugenia.”

Quickly, she turned out the light. She couldn’t believe she was holding a conversation with a ghost. And yet whenever she mentioned her name around the family, they weren’t surprised.

Desiree only smiled. This family knew about their ghost problem. They knew about Eugenia.

“Good night, Emily. Sleep well. Tomorrow is a new and exciting day. Now I’m going to visit Tanner.”

Emily laughed. Poor Tanner. After what she’d told the ghost, she would probably be giving him hell. And he didn’t believe in her. Too bad.

CHAPTER 13

What a night, and now all he wanted to do was close his eyes and dream about Emily. Turning the lights out, he snuggled beneath the covers and thought about the night. It had been so tempting to lay her back on the porch and do her right there beneath the stars.

The memory of their night together filled his mind and his hand reached down between his legs.

The smell of lavender filled the air and he jerked away. Just when he was going to enjoy himself, his mind started to play tricks on him. Not good. Not good at all.

"Tanner," the voice called as she appeared.

"Do you have to come unannounced into a man's bedroom?"

The woman laughed. "Yes, I do. We need to talk."

"My mind must be really sick. I'm thinking about Emily and you appear. Something is wrong."

The apparition hovered over his bed. Was she real? Really?

"Yes, there is," she said. "She's over in her cabin crying while she's telling me about her dead husband. She should be telling that to you."

"I've asked and she wouldn't tell me," he said. "Why am I talking to you about it. You're just a figment of my overactive mind. Now let me get some sleep."

"Not until I'm finished speaking to you."

"If I can somehow make you appear, I wish I knew how to make you disappear," he said, giving up and watching the apparition or whatever it was appear before him. If it was truly a ghost, that would be really kind of creepy.

The thing, whatever it was, shook her head. "You have no control over me. None. I'm not part of your PT problem. I'm a *grandmother problem.*"

"PTSD," he corrected her. "A *grandmother problem?*"

Why was she making sense all of a sudden? Why did he feel like she really was real? Travis had seen her. Desiree said she was real. Tucker believed in her. Was he the only one who refused to admit the truth?

"Damn, you really are a ghost," he said.

"Finally, we're making progress," she said. "Now, you and Emily...she says you're the problem."

"Me?" he exclaimed. "What does she want from me? We could be friends if she'd agree."

"You two are the most exasperating couple I've dealt with. She says you don't want a relationship. Is that true?"

How strange that they were both confiding in a ghost. And the problem was he wanted to be more than friends but feared his PTSD. No one would ever understand that problem. Sometimes he didn't think the counselors he saw at the VA hospital understood what went on in his head.

"Tanner," the ghost said, her voice rising.

There was no way a ghost over one hundred years old was going to understand why he felt the way he did.

"Yes, it's true," he admitted.

"Why?"

"I'm sure if you've spoken to Emily, she told you," he said, knowing he was in trouble. Knowing she would never understand.

"I want to hear your reasoning. Not her interpretation of what you said."

Oh great. When did ghosts learn to do psychoanalysis? Even his doctor at the VA didn't psychoanalyze him or at least he didn't think he did.

How much should he tell her and how much, given her age, could she understand?

"Do you understand what PTSD is?"

"It has something to do with the war," she said. "You keep reliving the battles?"

"Yes and no," he said. "Anyone can have PTSD after a terrifying life event. A traumatic event. Something that they live in fear of happening to them again. Or something triggers it and they are right back there in the event. That's what happens to me."

Over and over, it was the same battles with the same outcomes. Just once, he'd like to see his dead friends rise from the battles and live again. Just once.

"Oh my," she said.

"Some people never get over it," he said, knowing that was what he feared. "For some people, it takes time, therapy, and drugs to help them learn how to cope with the disease."

She flew over to a chair and sat.

"I'm not willing to put anyone I care about through the trauma of seeing me have an episode. When I feel one coming on, I get away from our guests, but even that terrifies me. What if I react to something in front of them?" Shaking his head, he remembered the first time a child had seen him and how he'd frightened her.

The little girl had run to her mother sobbing and when he came out of it, he'd been heartbroken.

"I'm better off alone," he said, knowing it was the only solution.

The ghost rose over the bed. "No one is better off alone. You just need someone who understands, who knows how to live with your problem. Someone who can help you when you have one of these events."

Maybe so, but until he felt certain that he could have an episode without hurting someone he loved, he would remain alone.

Now, they'd both had a chance to say their thoughts and he was ready to go to sleep. He didn't need a matchmaking ghost staying in his bedroom while he closed his eyes.

"You got anything else to say?"

Her mouth dropped open and she almost growled at him. "You can be such an impertinent child. Your great-great-great-great uncle was the same way. Stubborn right up until the end. I still have plenty to say, but the question is are you going to listen to me?"

He gave a little laugh. "Probably not. I'm tired. I have to work tomorrow. Thank goodness Travis and Samantha are returning. Why don't you rest up, so you can bug them for a while?"

She laughed. "No need for me to bother them again. They'll soon be married."

"Travis said they were going to wait," he told her.

A giggle ensued from her. "That's what he says now. But that won't last long."

Why was that? He wanted to ask but knew that would open up a whole new line of questions that he didn't want to hear tonight.

"I'll just be glad when he's back, so he can run interference between me and Aunt Rose," he said.

Oh my God, he was talking to a ghost like they were friends. Confiding in her. Now he was certifiable crazy.

"Don't worry about Aunt Rose," she said. "You're my grandson and you have nothing to worry about regarding your place in the family business. If she bothers you, she'll have a lot of sleepless nights with me singing her to sleep with an off-key rendition of 'Buffalo Gals, Won't You Come Out Tonight.'"

The thought of his Aunt Rose being serenaded was enough to have him laughing out loud. Oh, he couldn't wait to tell his brothers about this conversation. They would all enjoy how the ghost planned on getting even with their aunt.

"Now, you get your rest. Tomorrow is a new day with

new opportunities. I think you should ask Emily out on a date."

With everything that was going on at the ranch in the next few days, that wasn't going to be possible and he didn't need the entire family sticking their nose into his business. Or his Aunt Rose sending him a nasty gram via email. She'd done that before.

"Not happening," he said quietly. "I need to keep away from her. This thing whatever it is needs to end."

The ghost threw her hands up. "Just when I think I'm making progress with you, you disappoint me. This date is going to happen, even if it has to be a date neither of you planned on."

He wouldn't tell her that could not happen. But he would do his best to avoid Emily. Only problem was he had to convince his heart that she was off-limits and that was going to be hard to do.

CHAPTER 14

The next morning, Tanner couldn't resist going to the kitchen to check on Emily. Eugenia said she visited her last night. He wanted to learn what they had spoken about.

Walking into the kitchen, he saw she was making bread. There was flour on the table and she was kneading the dough in a large stainless-steel bowl.

"Good morning," he said. "What are you making?"

"Rolls, if they will rise like I want them to," she said. "It takes several hours."

He walked up close to her and breathed in the soft fragrance she wore. "You smell so good."

"Thank you," she said, continuing to knead the dough. "What do you need?"

"Did Eugenia come and speak to you last night?"

A frown appeared on her face, drawing her brows together. Her sapphire eyes darkened and a spiral of desire slithered down his spine.

"Yes," she said

"Did you talk about me?"

Somehow he had to keep his focus on their discussions with the ghost and not how he'd like to spread her across that table and take advantage of her.

"Not much," she said. "Mainly she listened while I explained how we cannot be together."

Why did it seem that her not wanting him made him want her more? There was this urgent need to show her that she couldn't live without him, and yet he knew that wouldn't be fair of him.

But, oh, how he wanted to kiss her. How he longed to cover her mouth with his and explore every inch of her.

"Did she agree?"

"No, I don't think so. I finally told her that I had to get some sleep so I wouldn't be so tired this morning."

For days, he'd been considering apologizing and had resisted and waited. But today seemed like the time for him to finally tell her he'd been wrong to act like he had. It had been a protective move to keep himself safe from her and he'd handled the situation poorly.

Picking up her hand, he stared into her sapphire eyes knowing he wanted things to be different between them. "I'm sorry about how I reacted to you being here. I'm sorry for how I've treated you. Can we be friends?"

He pulled her closer to him and she didn't resist. Maybe the kiss last night had softened her up to him. He hoped so, though he knew he would still not accept her as a girlfriend. But he could be her friend.

She leaned back and smiled at him. "Wow, an apology. I'm impressed."

"You should be," he said, his head naturally moving to the side as if he moved to kiss her. He longed to taste her and he would not be denied.

Suddenly the kitchen door swung open. "Tanner, there you are."

His brother Travis walked into the kitchen and grinned at him. "Come see me when you're finished."

"Oh, he's finished," Emily said, stepping back. "I've got to get back to my bread. It needs to rise for four hours."

Tanner dropped her hands, the spell broken.

"You were at the interview," she said.

"Yes, we met then," Travis said. "I'm glad to see you're here."

"Me too," she said and turned her back on Tanner dismissing him. Whatever mood they'd had dissipated. There would be no kiss now. Maybe not ever, but he'd wanted one so badly.

With a sigh, he ran his hand through his hair and walked toward Travis. "Let's go. There is a lot I need to catch you up on. Aunt Rose wants to fire me."

"What? This I need to hear."

Walking out of the kitchen, they headed to the office where they could talk about what had happened in the last week.

Travis turned to Tanner with a grin. "What's going on with you and the new cook?"

"I'll tell you when we reach the office. Let's just say my one-night stand followed me home."

Travis's eyes widened and he laughed. "Has Eugenia gotten involved?"

"Oh, yes. I did everything I could not to believe in her, but finally, I just gave up."

"She can wear on you," Travis said. "Look out, little brother, you could be getting married before me."

The thought terrorized him.

"Oh no, that's never going to happen."

It was after lunch before he had a chance to get back to the kitchen.

Once again, she was making bread. Now she was rolling out the dough and then cutting the rolls from the main dough ball.

When he walked in, she glanced up. "You can't seem to stay away."

"We need to talk," he said.

"About me leaving?" she asked.

"No, not about that," he said. "I've been thinking. We need to get our stories straight for Eugenia."

He glanced around. "You know she's doing her best to matchmake us. She told me that you don't want to get remarried and I'm not wanting anything permanent, so we need to do something to throw her off."

The woman laughed at him and wiped her hands on a towel hanging off her apron. Flour was spread over the stainless-steel table and floor as she rolled the dough and then cut off enough for a roll.

"What are you proposing," she asked, smiling as she put two pans of rolls to rise in the oven.

He'd been thinking about this all morning and

wondered if it would work. It could fool the ghost and give them each what they wanted. Their freedom.

But would it cure his insatiable need to be deep inside Emily?

"I think we play along with her schemes and make her think that we're a couple, but in reality, we're just doing this to make her happy. Then we'll have a big emotional break-up and tell her it just didn't work out."

Emily frowned at him. "But what is to keep her from trying to match us with other people?"

The thought of Emily with someone else sent a pang of jealousy through him. For a second, it made him tense as the effects rendered him immobile.

"The plan hasn't evolved that far. For now, let's just let her think we're together," he said, knowing he would have a hard time thinking of her with another man. Any man.

The smell of lavender filled the kitchen. Oh no, had she been here the entire time while they talked about how to fool her? That could be disastrous.

A big bowl rose into the air and slammed down on the ground, sounding like a gunshot, yanking him back to Iraq.

The sounds of gunfire were all around him and he flung himself to the side to miss a rocket flying over his head.

His buddy was standing beside him. "That was close."

"Watch out," he screamed and covered his friend's body to save him from the bullets flying. Brandon had been hit and Tanner knew he was next. They would circle back and kill him. Somehow he had to hide or play dead.

Hands were touching him. Cool, soft fingers were stroking his face and he heard her voice in the distance.

"Tanner, come back to me. You're safe. I'm protecting you. Nothing can hurt you here."

He gazed around. Blood was everywhere. His buddy lay motionless beneath him. Dear God, not Brandon. The man was dead.

Then he heard her voice softly singing to him, calling him to come home. "Tanner, Tanner, we're in the kitchen. You're not in Iraq any longer. Come back to me. Your home."

He shook his head and slowly the battlefield disappeared. He realized he was lying on the floor under a table. Emily was on him, holding down his arms, gazing into his eyes with the sweetest expression.

And then he felt her. Her breasts were crushed into his chest, her mound was snug against his rock-hard cock.

That had never happened in battle before.

Dumbfounded, he gazed up at her and knew she was the most beautiful woman he'd ever experienced in his life. She had brought him out of the battle. Something no one else had been able to do.

Her hands relaxed on his arms and he grabbed her face, bringing her lips down to his. He had to taste her, he had to have her. He couldn't wait another minute.

Desperation had him clinging to her. Greedily, his lips covered hers with an insistence that clawed at him. She saved him. The very moment, he'd been dreading was thrust upon him when she saw his PTSD up close and personal.

And she called to him in battle and carried him home.

Now because of how she'd soothed him, he had to have

her. He was filled with an urgency that surged through his blood, thundering in his ears, reverberating through his mind. This woman who tempted him, tantalized him, and soothed him, he wanted.

He had to have her now.

Right in this room with the flour rising and falling, he couldn't wait.

His mouth plundered hers as he melded her sweet body to his. His hands were everywhere as his need exploded through him in a gripping sensation. He needed her in a blinding way. He needed her to chase the demons from his consciousness and clear the voices from his mind. He needed her to rescue him from the battlefields in his head.

Her mouth opened up like a flower, and his tongue caressed the inside of her lip, then swept her mouth, insistent and urgent. She wrapped her arms around his neck and clung to him, pressing her sweet body against him, seeking what he was more than happy to supply.

No, it wasn't the best place to have sex, but this was a desire that had to be fulfilled right here and right now.

Shifting her clothing, he pulled her pants down and she grabbed his belt undoing the buckle and finding the zipper. When she pulled it down, his cock sprang out and she wrapped her loving hands around his organ.

"Oh God," he cried, knowing he wouldn't last long not like this.

His hand skimmed down the front of her chef coat, cupping her breast, kneading the soft mound while he ached to wrap his lips around her sweet nipple.

She tasted of erotic dreams and lazy mornings, and

everything he tried to withhold from himself. But not today. Not when his need was this crucial. Now when he couldn't wait.

She pulled his mouth back to her lips, collecting his attention once again, while kissing him hungrily.

At any moment, someone could walk into the kitchen and find them having sex in the flour under the table, but he didn't care. Right now all he could think about was being inside Emily. Of her carrying him over the next ridge until they were both satisfied.

He opened her chef coat wider and unhooked her bra. A moan escaped her throat as his mouth caressed her sweet breast.

"Uh-uh. Lose your pants," she indicated with a wave of her hand.

"With pleasure," he gasped as he raised just enough to slide his pants down to his ankles, where they would have to stay. Because he wasn't moving until they were both satisfied. He feared she would come to her senses and it would all come to a crashing end.

And he needed her too much to risk that happening.

He glanced into her gaze; the fire in her eyes scorched him, and he clenched his fists needing to be inside her now.

Gently, he cupped the center of her core while his lips nibbled on her earlobe. His fingers brushed her satiny folds, tempting and teasing while his lips brushed her neck, trailing down her creamy shoulders, sampling her sweet flesh. Her lashes fluttered and he could feel her pulse beneath his lips pounding rhythmically.

Her lips were too tempting as he covered them once again. He didn't want to talk right now. He only wanted to feel, to experience this woman.

The floor was hard, but he lifted her over him, placing his penis at the juncture of her thighs.

“Fuck me,” he groaned.

"Oh, Tanner," she whispered in his ear as his fingers delved into her moist depths, preparing her. Needing to be deep inside her.

To feel her body lying on his. Feel her flesh wrapped around him, pulsing against him. No thoughts of tomorrow, no thoughts of the next five minutes, only this moment, the two of them pursuing the desire between them.

With a primal surge, he entered her, needing to feel her surrounding him, burying himself deep within her.

Her soft whimpers of pleasure increased with each long, slow stroke of his body as he lifted her up and down on his cock.

Emily had changed him, made him see life from a different angle. Made him realize just how empty his existence had been until she'd stumbled into his world. In one week, she had turned his life upside down and he was confused as to where they went from here.

His lips covered hers as they shared the breath of life, his nostrils filled with the scent of Emily, the taste of Emily on his lips. And he was consumed with a passion that surpassed anything he'd ever felt.

He clasped her hands in his, bracing against her, plunging deeper and deeper into her, feeling as if his soul was joining with hers. Her eyelashes fluttered against her cheek. Her body quivered as she shuddered with completion.

"Tanner," she whispered, and his heart swelled. God, this woman had a way of making him feel larger than life.

He couldn't hold back any longer. He'd waited as long as he could, but Emily was ready. Together they reached that pinnacle once again. Only this time, they were covered in flour fallen from the tabletop.

As they slowly came down, he felt her tense and knew she realized what they had just done. Dear God, they could be caught at any moment as they lay there in each other's arms.

CHAPTER 15

Lying on top of Tanner under the stainless-steel table in the kitchen, she took a deep breath. What the hell had she just done?

Was she totally out of her mind? And yet it seemed right. When he kissed her and they started ripping at each other's clothes, the moment had been perfect.

They were partially unclothed with nothing but a swinging door separating them from the dining hall. The place where they held the arts and crafts classes, the dance lessons, the card games. People were all around them and anyone could walk in at any second.

And if they were discovered, she was certain she would be fired.

Their joining had been urgent and insistent and something neither one wanted, and yet they couldn't get enough of each other.

When Tanner started into his hallucination, she'd instinctively reacted like she did when John had one. And her soothing voice and singing brought him back. If she could get close enough, touch also helped, but she had learned to be observant. Sometimes they thought you were the enemy.

Tanner had responded to her touch and her voice and he'd come back once she climbed under the table and covered his body with hers. Singing to him and calling him, telling him she was here and she needed him.

And, oh, how she needed him.

At the sound of her voice, Tanner instantly reached for her and somehow they found themselves tearing at each other's clothing, trying to get to one another's flesh. It had been a frenzied act where they could not touch one another fast enough.

Where she craved the feel of his skin against hers.

Oh no, it hadn't just been Tanner, it had been the two of them. And now, how did she get out of this awkward situation? Had her brain turned to mush and all logical thinking dissolved at his touch?

It certainly felt that way. Because she had wanted him as badly as he desired her.

His breathing had returned to normal and she didn't want to look at him for fear of the loathing she would see there. For fear of how they now would handle this indiscretion.

He'd made it very clear that he wanted nothing to do with her, and yet, here they were. Almost naked, spread out on the floor beneath the flour for her bread, she just had the most mind-numbing unbelievable sex of her life.

Had it been the same for him?

"We better get dressed and clean this mess up," Tanner said.

A chill scurried down her spine at his words.

There was no mention of his episode. There was no mention of them having the most amazing sex she'd ever experienced. Oh no, it was *hide the evidence and do it now before we get caught.*

Rolling from under the table, her feet hit the floor. She ached in places she'd forgotten all about. People didn't have sex on concrete because it was hard and uncomfortable, even being on top.

Straightening her clothes, she glanced down at her chef's coat and saw the flour clinging to it, and her black pants were dusted like a fine crepe. Tanner didn't look much better. The back of his shirt was covered and his jeans had a fine coating of white powder.

"Let me brush you off," she said. So far, he'd said barely eight words to her and while she didn't expect roses, a little acknowledgment would be wonderful. A little *it was good for me, was it good for you?*

A *thank you for helping*. Anything besides this cold man who didn't want to acknowledge what had just happened between them. This explosion of heat and sensuality they had ridden to the moon and back on.

He turned, and as he was tucking his shirt into his jeans, she brushed the white powder off the back of his shirt as best she could.

Now fully clothed with everything in the right place, he faced her and she could see he wanted to say something.

Damn it, why had she let this happen again? Because she had witnessed pain like this before and it just seemed natural to comfort him. To help him escape from the images in his mind.

But sex?

"I didn't hurt you, did I?"

Not physically, but the emotional toll she was afraid would come as soon as he left.

"No," she said. "John used to have the same type of episodes where suddenly he was fighting a battle. Is that what happens to you?"

"Yes," he said. "Did you sing to me?"

She gave a little laugh. "Yes, it always soothed and brought John out of the battle."

A battle that eventually he returned to, but still when they were together, it helped him come back to her. Just like it had brought Tanner to her. A hot, very desperate-for-sex Tanner who she had wanted just as much.

And that frightened her.

Was that the smart thing to do, when she knew he didn't want her?

With soft eyes, he stared at her. "Someday you need to tell me about him."

"Someday," she said, walking across the room and grabbing a broom, where she began to sweep up the flour. It was useless since she had not cleaned off the table, but she'd do anything to be in motion and stop the thoughts rattling in her brain about how this man didn't want her.

And yet, she'd just had the best sex of her life. Damn.

More restless energy filled her, so she grabbed the cleaning rag and began to tackle the table, sweeping off the flour to the floor.

Desiree and Travis walked into the kitchen. They stopped in the doorway and gazed at the flour-covered table and the two of them with a coating of bleached dust clinging to them.

"What happened?" Desiree asked, her large emerald eyes wide with disbelief. "You're both covered in white powder."

"Flour," Emily said.

Travis gave a snicker and Emily knew he understood.

"Is dinner going to be served on time," Desiree asked, suddenly concerned.

"Of course," Emily said sharply as she gazed at the people in her kitchen. Why wouldn't they leave? She had work to do. Tears bubbled up in her throat that needed to be shed.

Tears for being so stupid to let a man who didn't want her have his way with her again. For being so stupid to jeopardize everything for ten minutes of pure pleasure.

She needed time alone. She needed to think about what just happened. This time, the sex between her and Tanner had been quick, insistent, and demanding.

And dang, why did it feel like he was a missing part of her?

Why was the sex so wonderful and he was such a pain in the ass?

"Everyone out," she said. "I've got to clean this mess up. I've got work to do."

"What happened? Did something explode?"

Yes, two people exploded on the floor and it was wonderful and so frustrating at the same time. What was she supposed to say?

Travis covered his mouth and she could see he was trying not to laugh. But he understood what had transpired here.

"Make sure you clean the area real well," he said laughing.

Emily glared at him. Tanner said nothing, but she could see how uneasy he was.

"I've got work to do. All of you out," she said. "You too, Tanner."

She could see that he wanted to talk, but she was in no mood at this point. That time had long passed and he'd said nothing. The episode had happened so suddenly. What had triggered him?

A gasp escaped her and she knew. "Eugenia."

"Eugenia, what?" Desiree asked, looking very confused.

"She caused this," Emily said.

Tanner frowned at her. "How?"

"Just before your attack began that pan on the floor over there flew into the air and dropped."

Travis glanced at Tanner. "You had another episode?"

"Yes," he said quietly.

"And then what happened?" Travis said.

"That is none of your business," Tanner said and walked out of the kitchen, leaving her to deal with these two.

Just like him to run when things became a problem. And she was most definitely a problem for him.

Desiree glanced at Travis and then back to Emily. "Strange things are going on. Are you certain you don't need help cleaning up?"

That was the last thing Emily wanted. Right now, she just needed everyone to leave, so she could think about what had transpired between her and Tanner and her feelings.

Tears welled in her eyes.

"Are you all right?" Desiree asked.

"I'm fine. Please check on Tanner. Make certain he's all right. Make certain he is not having another episode. Sometimes they come back to back."

Why wouldn't these people get out of her kitchen? She just wanted to be alone.

Travis stepped up to her. "Emily, if you helped him through his flashback, that's something none of us have been able to do."

Taking a deep breath, she glanced up at Tanner's brother. "My husband used to suffer from PTSD, so I know what helped him. But, please, this brought up old memories for me. I just need a few minutes alone."

Standing there staring at the mess in the beautiful kitchen, she watched them leave and then the tears fell in earnest. Putting her face in her hands, she cried.

Tanner and John were nothing alike. And yet, here she was falling in love with the soldier who suffered from a mind-shattering illness just like John. She didn't want to fall in love again.

When she left Colorado, she wanted a new beginning, but she had not wanted a man in her life right now. And she certainly didn't want another soldier. But here she was, and as much as she didn't want to, she could feel herself falling in love with Tanner.

Damn him. All she wanted to do was cook, and yet, her heart was becoming attached.

And he didn't want her. That hurt more than anything.

CHAPTER 16

Tanner all but ran out of the kitchen, thankful that Emily had told them all to leave. The others had stayed, but he was walking as fast as he could in any direction away from what transpired back there.

Fear spiraled through him like a swirling tornado eating up everything in its path, sending him running from life and all that happened this morning.

Never had he come out of an episode in the arms of a woman and all he'd wanted was for her to make him forget about the battle he'd experienced again. To heal him from the wounds he suffered internally. To make him feel alive and loved. And she'd been right there.

Convenient, accessible, and so damn intoxicatingly sexy that he'd just reacted, seeking his release and to find fulfillment in her arms. Fulfillment at any cost.

Anyone could have walked in on them at any time, but he didn't care. It was like he'd become obsessed with getting inside her and nothing could've stopped him. In some ways, he felt like a bull in heat.

Thank goodness his brother and Desiree had not arrived five minutes earlier or they would have witnessed them doing it right there in the kitchen, with puffs of flour rising as they moved with only one destination, nirvana.

It had not been like the night at the hotel where afterward they'd cuddled and spoken such sweet words to each other. Oh no, this had been nothing but pure sex, and afterward, he didn't know what to say.

Awkward was the only word that came to mind, but yet he'd never felt such relief. Such passion, such enjoyment in a woman's arms. Pleasure had exploded around them and he'd been whisked away.

Thank you, seemed so cold. But still, he should have said something, and now she probably hated him even more for the way he had used her and walked away.

"Tanner," he heard his brother's voice, but he didn't want to stop. Travis knew what went on in that kitchen and he would expect an explanation.

What could he say? He didn't know what to say to Emily. And he didn't want to talk to Travis. All he wanted was to be alone.

Suddenly he heard his brother's footsteps.

"Wait up, I'm too old to run in this heat," he said, huffing and puffing.

Tanner stopped and gazed at Travis.

"Go away."

"No," Travis said. "Are you all right?"

"I'm fine," he said, knowing his brother spoke about the episode he'd experienced. Never had one been so short. But Emily had brought him back, and for that he was thankful.

They walked along in silence.

"Where are we going?"

"Don't know," Tanner said, realizing he'd just been walking as fast as he could to escape what had happened in the kitchen. To escape the feelings that Emily seemed to evoke in him. The feelings of protectiveness and the way he wanted to shield her from the speculation he feared they would soon face.

Oh, how life would have been so much easier if she'd left the day she arrived, but now, he didn't want her to leave. But could he learn to live with her here?

"It's kind of hot to be out taking a walk," Travis said.

"Yes, it is, but I have to get away," he said.

"You can't run from your feelings," Travis said softly. "I know. I tried."

His brother had been running from women since his first wife and child were killed in a tragic car accident. But now he was happy with Samantha. And Tanner was so excited for the two of them.

Yet, that didn't mean he was next. Eugenia could learn to live with the fact that one of her grandsons was not going to be married. Just no. It was time for her to move on to the next appointed grandson.

"How's Samantha doing? Does she like living at the ranch?"

Somehow he needed to change the topic and get off him and Emily.

"She's settling in," he said. "She's rearranging the house to her satisfaction and I don't care. If it makes her happy, then that's all that's important."

Tanner glanced at his brother and smiled.

"I'm happy for you two," he said.

"You could have that same happiness," Travis said. "All you have to do is stop running from those feelings."

In some ways, he knew his older sibling was right, but there was still this damn PTSD. And they were back to speaking about him.

"You know that's not possible for me. Look what happened today. I had an episode, and bam, I'm doing the help."

That was not fair because Emily was so much more than just the help, but he couldn't express any feelings right now.

Travis started laughing, his eyes twinkling as he gazed at Tanner. "I'm going to have a hard time not looking at that table and thinking about what occurred under there."

"I owe her a big apology," Tanner said. "She brought me back from the battlefield and it was like I lost all control. The next thing I know, we're yanking at each other's clothing and then I was... We could have gotten caught."

A grin spread across his brother's face. "But you didn't. Though it was close. Poor Desiree has no idea what happened, but from looking at the two of you, I knew exactly what occurred. You both looked like you rolled in flour, your eyes were bright and shiny and your faces pink. And your breathing was a little hurried. I hope it was really good."

With a sigh, Tanner closed his eyes. "The best. And yet I ran out of there like a scared little boy."

Emily deserved better. He'd failed her once again.

"Tanner, this is the most excited I've ever seen you about a woman," Travis said. They had stopped walking and were standing beneath one of the big elm trees on the property.

"Just take it slow. Don't push her away, but rather get to know her. It's been a fast two weeks since you met her."

"Less than that," Tanner said, thinking back to how much he'd enjoyed that time at the hotel with her. And today, how he'd needed her to hold him, love him, and make him whole again.

And she had done just that.

That was the problem, so far, she was the perfect woman for him and that terrified him.

"Samantha and I fell in love in a week's time, only it took me a lot longer to realize it."

Tanner remembered that time not so long ago when Travis was falling for the ghost hunter. Was he falling in love with Emily? No, he couldn't.

But maybe it was possible, and maybe, just maybe, he could learn to love again. She knew how to deal with someone who had PTSD. She hadn't been afraid. She'd stayed with him, not giving up, but trying to calm him. No one had ever done that for him.

Leaving like he did without saying anything, had he screwed everything up?

Squatting on his ankles, he grabbed his head.

"I should have said something to her, but I didn't know

what to say. And then you guys barged into the kitchen, just as I finished zipping my fly. *Thank you for the fuck* seemed so wrong because it was so much more. But I can't tell her I love her. I can't say much of anything except that I was grateful for how she handled my episode today. I was grateful for how she held me in her arms."

A cow mooed at them as they were not far from the gate to the pasture. Slowly Tanner stood.

"That's a start," Travis said. "But you're right. Women like to be held and cuddled after sex and you didn't have time for that. Tonight, you need to make up for what happened. Talk to her and tell her how you're feeling."

Confused? He should tell her that he was feeling tangled, torn, and so afraid of what he could be walking away from. So afraid of taking a chance with her and failing. So afraid of hurting her with one of his flashes.

"All right," he said, knowing he had to talk to her. Tonight, sitting out on her porch, maybe she'd be in her pajamas again. "Maybe she'll talk to me about her husband," he said. "What if I knew him?"

"Doubtful," Travis said. "Besides, don't bring up her husband. Let her mention him. Just be kind and thoughtful and tell her that today meant a lot to you. Unless it didn't."

"No, it did," Tanner said. "That's what's so scary. Today, it was like everything came together and what we did was almost binding. It felt like we were meant to be together. To help one another. And I've never experienced that before."

"Take her some flowers." Travis clapped him on the back. "Welcome to love, brother."

"No, I can't love her," Tanner said, fear spiking through him.

"Well, it sure sounds like love. You don't have to tell her right now. You can wait and see if this is the real thing."

With a deep breath, Tanner gazed at Travis suddenly realizing that he and Desiree had been searching for him. "Why did you come into the kitchen?"

"The men are out hunting the bull. Seems he tore down a fence to get at one of the cows. See what love can do to you? You were kind of like that bull today. You had to get to your woman."

Tanner shook his head. "We can't have a rodeo tomorrow without a bull."

"Nope, we can't. That is unless you'd like to take his place." A grin spread across Travis's face. "Come on, little brother. We've got work to do."

"Ha-ha," Tanner said as they walked back to the house. "Very funny. Me being the bull."

"If the horns fit…"

CHAPTER 17

Emily was lying in bed reading the same page of a book over and over, her mind rethinking about what had happened today. No matter how much she tried, she couldn't concentrate on the story. All she could do was think about the incredible sex they had in the kitchen.

How in the world she could have let herself get so carried away that not only did she have sex with Tanner, but it had been unprotected sex? Unprotected, no birth control, no disease control, nothing but her man and her having the best sex she'd ever experienced.

Glancing at the calendar, she knew she was at her most fertile time and she only hoped that the way they had jumped up after they were finished, that the sperm had not made its way to her egg. But she knew that was wishful thinking. Time would tell.

While she would love to have a child and a family of her own, that was not a good way to start a relationship. And Tanner couldn't handle being with her, let alone a child. He was not the person to start a family with, no matter how much she wanted one.

It was best not to worry about it until she knew for certain, so for now, she would push it out of her mind and instead concentrate on how she'd felt so close to Tanner.

The sex had been wonderful. But afterward, it was like he'd run scared out of the kitchen. Especially when his brother and cousin appeared at the door.

With a sigh, she thought how she'd cleaned up the kitchen, prepared the bread, the salads, and the main entree before finally going to her cabin and collapsing.

Everything had gone smoothly except that her heart was in tatters. Today she recognized the feelings growing for Tanner and that frightened her.

The sound of a knock on her door had her sliding out of bed. If he was here for sex, he could kiss her rosy-red cheeks. Not going to happen.

When she went to the door, she peeked out the window and saw him standing there impatiently. Part of her didn't want to answer the door, yet she had to know what he wanted.

Pulling back the latch, she opened the door and stared at him, not saying a word.

"These are for you," he said and handed her a bouquet of wildflowers.

Speechless, she stared at them. They were beautiful and yet she felt like a hypocrite for accepting them. She'd been angry with him all afternoon. Furious because after they had sex, he left never even acknowledging what they had just done.

"Why don't you put them in water and then come outside and talk to me," he said.

He wasn't trying to push his way inside and that made her feel a little better.

"Just a moment," she said.

Walking back inside, she left the door open, testing to see if he would push his way in, but instead he sat on the steps.

Obviously he must have known how upset she'd been after he left her this afternoon.

After she put the flowers in water, she came back outside, once again in her pajamas. Sinking down on the step beside him, she didn't say a word.

"Thank you for helping me this afternoon," he said, reaching out and taking her hand. "No one has ever gotten through to me when I'm having one of my episodes."

"You're welcome," she said softly.

She could see there was something else he wanted to say but was struggling to speak the words.

"I also want to apologize for jumping up after we had sex and running out the door. I was stunned at how we both reacted and at how unbelievably good it was. Nothing has ever happened like that before with me. One minute, I was fighting the war, and the next minute, you were in my arms."

So he had been affected just like she had been by what happened between them. She closed her eyes and felt the tears welling inside. There was no way she could avoid it any longer. She was falling for him and that terrified her.

"It was so quick and yet so incredibly satisfying," she said.

And she'd also realized just how much she cared for him. This afternoon had been incredible.

Turning to face her, he placed his hands on her cheeks. "You're an amazing woman and I want you so badly, but I'm afraid. So afraid of hurting you when I'm in the middle of a hallucination. So afraid you'll get tired of my problem and walk away from me. Who wants a cripple for a husband? There's so much wrong with me that I can't believe a beautiful woman like you would want me."

His hands slipped away and she felt disappointed that he did not kiss her. She'd wanted to feel his mouth on hers.

It was all she could not to reach out and slap him.

"You are not a cripple. Never call yourself that. With time, this could get better." Taking a deep breath, she leaned her head back, closed her eyes, and prayed for patience. So many did not understand what dealing with PTSD was like. And yet he lived with it.

"John had PTSD," she said, lifting her head and staring into his eyes. "At the oddest moments, he would suddenly have an episode. After reading up on it, I learned to talk calmly to him. To touch him, unless he grew violent. I learned that music, singing, often brought him back from the recess of his mind."

The memory of all the times she'd dealt with his hallucinations rushed toward her and she sighed. "It's a difficult disease."

"You're the first wife of a military veteran who has

experienced her husband's PTSD that I've spoken to. I'm curious to hear what you think about the disease."

"Hate it," she said. "Hated it for him. For me. Hated how it stole him from me."

"How was that?" Tanner asked.

"John loved being a soldier. And yet, after his second tour of duty in Iraq, I noticed a change in him. No longer was he the laughing, carefree man I had fallen in love with. Everything was by the rules. There was so little give and take with him. Before he was easygoing. And then I witnessed my first episode of PTSD. He shoved me onto the floor, covered my body, and was protecting me from *incoming*. Scared the crap out of me."

"I've experienced what you're talking about," Tanner said. "Did he die from an episode?"

Her face seemed to tighten and she shook her head.

"No, he was one of the last soldiers in Iraq. He was helping load refugees onto airplanes. He was gathering the information for them to get on the list to board when he saw a man with a bomb. Knocking him down, he covered him, dying when the jerk detonated the device."

Oh God, how she hated how he died, but knew he'd been doing what he loved and was a hero. Only she couldn't take being a hero's wife.

"They say he saved so many lives, but all I could think about was what our life together could have been. We had so many plans and dreams. But he saved women and children in Iraq, but he wasn't here to save me. Selfish, I know, but it's what drove me to leave Colorado."

"How's that?"

"If I tell you, it has to stay between us. The reason I left Colorado was to get away from people always reminding me what a wonderful man John was. Because of the constant outpouring of sympathy, I couldn't heal. I couldn't move on. When they dedicated a new Veterans Park, I was John's widow. When they did a toy drive, they invited me, John's widow. When they needed to raise money for a military charity, it was *ask John's widow*."

All the memories of attending so many military functions came rushing back. She had to get away.

"I couldn't heal. I couldn't get over John because everywhere I turned I was reminded of him. So that's why I decided to move. New place, new adventures."

Tanner pulled her closer to him. "Only you didn't plan on meeting another veteran, did you?"

"No," she said, *or falling in love with him*. But she would not tell him until she was certain this was going to be real. Right now, it felt tenuous. It could go either way, and either way, her heart would be broken.

They sat on the steps gazing at the stars. Touching side to side, shoulder to shoulder.

"I don't know if I will ever be a man who can make a commitment. I don't know if these episodes will ever disappear. Or if I'll be a man who can marry a woman and trust her to live with his demons. I'm just taking it day by day."

"That's all any of us can do," she said. "There is something between us. This afternoon proved that this attraction to one another is very powerful."

"Yes, it is," he said. "I'm willing to try. But we're going to take it slow. And no more kitchen sex."

A giggle erupted from her and warmth filled her. "I'd like to try. You have to remember that you're not the only one who has experienced this trauma. I may not live in the hallucinations and see the battlefield, but I've heard the screams, the cries, and lived with a soldier trying to protect me. None of this is easy."

"No, it's not," he said. "Anytime you want to tell me to go away, I understand."

They had made progress, but still, he didn't realize how that wasn't possible.

"That's the problem, Tanner," she said, pulling his face around, the urge to kiss him overwhelming her. "I'm so damn attracted to you that I tried to stay away from you, and today just showed me how wrong I'd been."

A grin spread across his face, and then she leaned in and kissed him. Her lips covered his as she melted against him. Eagerly his lips took control and he kissed her like she was his last breath of life. Like he would never let her go.

A slamming door had them separating, and she gazed into his emerald gaze, seeing the passion shining even in the dim light of her porch light. The day seemed to have sapped her strength and then she remembered how his episode began.

"And the next time your grandmother comes around. We're going to have words. She started your episode today and I'm going to end her thinking that sending you back to war is a good thing."

He laughed, his voice deep, and a vibration spiraled through her. There was something about his happiness that touched all her buttons.

"Good luck with that," he said. "But it did bring us together. I just hope she didn't stick around to watch us in the kitchen."

"Oh my," Emily said. "That would be an offense that would get her banned permanently from the ranch."

CHAPTER 18

Most of the time, Tanner enjoyed the rodeo. During the summer, it was put on once a week and some of the local cowboys came over to take advantage of the experience of riding a bull or roping a calf.

There was barrel racing for the kids, and overall, it was just a good time, and their guests loved it. Some of them even participated in the parade at the beginning and the end of the rodeo.

It was a guest-favorite event and even Tanner was having fun. Though sometimes the animals, especially the bull, gave them trouble.

Lucas, the old bull, could be a stubborn animal, but so far, he'd not hurt any of the riders. But that didn't mean there wouldn't be a first time, and they always advised their guests not to get too close to the fence surrounding the bleachers under their big top tent.

Every precaution was taken to make certain the riders

were safe. They even had a few clowns to distract the bull when he went after a cowboy that had been bucked off his back.

Hitting the dirt could stun you, but an eight-hundred-pound animal charging you had you moving quickly up and out of the arena.

Those dudes were as crazy as they came, though they loved to jump the fence to get away from the bull. Some of the clowns were daring in their approach to drawing the attention away from the fallen rider. And there were always two men on horseback that would intervene if needed.

Most of the time the two men on horseback escorted the bull to the gate after a ride and he went not giving them any trouble. But occasionally, he could be ornery. Occasionally, he resisted.

Tonight, Tanner was riding a horse and escorting old Lucas out of the arena. It was a job he enjoyed and one he could do without much stress.

The night was almost over. They had a parade and a salute to the flag at the beginning, then the barrel racers, the calf roping, and finally, they ended with the bull riding and the final parade around the arena.

People sat in the stands while the cowboys lined up to take their turn riding The Beast as he was affectionately called. Since he had been back in his section of fence and not out visiting the ladies, he should be spoiling for a fight tonight.

And the riders would love how the bull did its best to send them flying off its back.

"Next up is the bull riding," Tanner heard their announcer call. "Jet Randolph will be our first rider. His stats for the summer are three rides and one nosedive."

The crowd laughed. While they tried to make it seem like a real rodeo, the only people who saw the riders were the townsfolk who were invited to attend and the guests at the ranch. They were not professionals but locals.

His brother Travis's job was to make certain that the cowboys were safely on the animal and not trapped or pinned when the gate opened. He was the last set of eyes before they hovered over the top of the animal and took off when the alarm sounded.

This was a challenging and scary position to be in at the rodeo.

Glancing out into the crowd, Tanner saw Emily handing out cookies to the guests in the stands. Warmth filled his heart and he knew she took her job here very seriously. So far, their guests were raving about her cooking and even his Aunt Rose said they had found a gem.

The older woman was sitting in the stands tonight. Sometimes she attended, but often she stayed home. It was hard to believe she'd soon be seventy-eight, and the family would hold a big party for her.

One day, she would move out of the old house and give it to Travis and Samantha. Travis's woman sat in the stands and watched the rodeo. He said she was working on a documentary about ghosts but promised that nothing would be included about their great-great-great-great-grandmother. Though if a film would send her hightailing it back to the grave, that would be great. A relief for all the single Burnett men.

It was a warm summer night and the show was almost finished. All that was left was one more ride and then the closing ceremony. And he couldn't wait to spend some time with Emily.

In the last few days, they seemed to have reached an understanding, and he was happy. They were taking each day as it came and enjoying being together.

Emily finished handing out cookies and was coming down the stairs of the stands. Tonight, he planned on going back to her place and sitting outside with her on the porch. They would have to battle mosquitos, but it would be nice to hold her hand, steal a few kisses, and talk about their dreams, their wishes, and what they wanted in life. Mainly, it would be nice to spend time together.

Next up was the last rider. The gate opened. The bull came charging out of the gate with the rider on its back. It flipped and jumped and did everything it could to toss the cowboy into the dirt.

Watching closely, Tanner realized the rider's hand was stuck under the rope and he couldn't release safely.

Furious that the man still rode its back, the bull headed to the fence surrounding the arena to knock him off. When crashing head-on into the wood, the planks made a loud cracking noise and the fence collapsed. The rider finally released, flying up and out of the way. But the bull had gained its freedom, escaping into the area surrounding the bleachers.

All the men jumped down off the fence and raced toward the animal.

Emily stood frozen, staring as a ton of pure animal muscle charged her.

Dear God, no.

Tanner kicked the sides of his horse and galloped full speed toward her. He prayed no one would step in front of his horse as he sprinted to her side knowing if the bull gored her with its horns, she'd be killed. There stood the woman he loved with all his heart and soul, and he couldn't live without her.

His heart was pounding as he leaned over and scooped an arm around her ribs, snatching her up, and rode away.

"Tanner," she cried.

"Damn, Emily, you know how to give a man a heart attack."

The bull raced out of the pavilion, heading to his pasture. Obviously, he'd had enough of being ridden for one day. Tanner felt relief at seeing him gallop away.

"Are you all right?"

"Yes," she said, breathless. "I've never been so scared. What happened?"

"He broke the fence around the arena trying to get a cowboy off his back. You just happened to be in his path."

Cheers rose from the crowd as Tanner rode back into the arena with Emily in his arms. It felt good to be holding her close to his chest. He didn't want to let her go.

She held onto Tanner, holding him tight, her body shaking. "I thought I was going to die."

He didn't say the words he thought because they would have confirmed her fear.

Travis and several other cowboys rode out of the pavilion on horses to catch the loose bull. He was a danger to anyone who got in his way and they had guests outside the arena.

"Everyone please remain in your seats until we receive the all-clear," the announcer said.

"Another couple of seconds and he would have reached me," Emily said.

"But he didn't," Tanner said. "You're safe. I'm not going to let anything hurt you."

Tanner continued to hold Emily in his arms as she continued to shake. He rode behind the tent and a ranch hand grabbed the horse's bridle.

"Good work, Tanner," he said. "Ms. Emily, are you all right?"

"I'm okay," she said though she sounded breathless and frightened to Tanner.

The cowboy helped her off the horse and then Tanner swung his leg over and dropped down beside her.

For a moment, he took her into his arms and she clung to him. He could feel her trembling.

He looked up and glanced into his Aunt Rose's eyes. Standing over to the side, she frowned at him. She walked up to where they stood.

"Emily, are you all right?"

"Yes, ma'am," she said, stepping out of Tanner's embrace, her hands still quivered. "Though, I was plenty scared."

Tanner could see his aunt was carefully checking them out. He could see that she no longer believed they were fighting. She could see they were a couple.

"All of us were," she said. She tilted her head and gazed at the two of them. "You two make a cute couple. Tanner, my office, eight o'clock in the morning. Emily, I'll expect you at nine o'clock with next week's menus. Don't disappoint me."

"Yes, ma'am," Emily said. "Tanner is going to walk me home."

A grin spread across Tanner's face. One thing about Emily, she didn't back down, and she was letting his aunt know they were indeed a couple. Tomorrow morning, he would be grilled and probably warned not to run off her favorite chef.

The older woman grinned. "See you both in the morning."

The woman was about to walk out of the pavilion and one of the guards stopped her. "You can't leave."

Oh, the poor man must be new and didn't know who she was. Tanner pitied him.

"The hell I can't. I'm getting in that truck over there and if that beast comes after me, I'll run him over. Save all of us a lot of trouble. And if he kills me, be sure to send him to the glue factory."

The man laughed. "I'll walk you to your truck, Miss Rose."

"Now, that, I would appreciate."

Tanner watched as his aunt leaned on her cane to reach her truck, then he turned to Emily.

"She's not going to fire me," he said.

"No, I won't let her," Emily said. "Besides, didn't you say Eugenia threatened to sing to her if she fired you?"

"Yes," he said laughing.

"No worries," she said. "Take me home. I need you. That was too close a call."

"Gladly," he said. "As soon as they catch the beast and it's safe to leave the pavilion, we'll go back to your cabin."

CHAPTER 19

When they reached Emily's cabin, she pulled him through the door. Instantly they were on one another and she tried to remember if she'd ever felt such instantaneous passion before.

Never.

Just the smell of Tanner had her senses alert. The touch of his hand had her stomach clenching and a spiral of heat building inside her. Just a look from him could make her body react.

He pulled her against his chest and his lips covered hers in a kiss that was demanding and she surrendered. After tonight, she needed his arms around her, protecting her, loving her.

Tonight, she'd looked into that bull's eyes and known she was going to die. And then Tanner's arms were sweeping her up, his horse galloping them away from the danger. Clinging to him, she realized he saved her from certain death.

Releasing his lips, she pulled him to the bed in the little cabin.

His fingers were on the buttons of her chef's coat and then he was pushing it down her arms. Pulling his shirt from his jeans, she fumbled with the buttons trying to get to his skin. Pausing, she ran her hands on his well-muscled chest, loving the feel of his heartbeat beneath her fingers.

Just the feel of his flesh had her heart racing and her breathing quickening before she pulled down the sleeves of his shirt. It dropped to the floor alongside her chef coat.

His fingers were at the waistband of her pants and she quickly kicked off the flats she wore.

Reaching for his belt buckle, she undid the clasp, and then flicked the button on his jeans before she pulled his zipper down.

"Emily," he said. "You make me feel like a sixteen-year-old kid dreaming of his first girl."

She chuckled. "Don't you dare go off too fast on me."

"Never," he said with a chuckle. "But you better get my pants down."

"Your boots are in the way," she said.

With a groan, he sank onto the bed and yanked his boots off then shucked his jeans. They landed on the floor with a *thunk*.

He reached for her pants and slid them down while she unhooked her bra. His underwear landed in the same pile of clothes.

Finally, they were naked.

He pulled her between his knees, his mouth going to

her nipples. As he sucked the orb into his mouth, she clung to him. How could this simple act bring so much pleasure?

She pushed him back until he fell onto the bed, but then he rolled her over onto her back.

There was no hesitation as she moved her hands down his warm skin. She wanted to run her hands all over him, and she wanted his hands to touch her. She needed to feel his bare skin against hers.

Never before had she felt this urgent need. A sense that she would go up in flames at any moment. Oh, how she loved the feeling of being beneath him. Of knowing they would soon be joining.

Her breathing sounded harsh, but she couldn't get enough air; she couldn't stop her racing heart. She couldn't control this urge for him to be inside her, joining her, melding her, making her his.

His fingers found her center and teased her. "Tanner!"

"Oh God, yes," he said as he kissed her, his mouth trailing kisses down her stomach until he reached her very center.

When his mouth closed over her, she moaned as pleasure skyrocketed through her. Her fingers found his hair, and she clasped his head. He lifted her hips until his mouth was firmly planted on her center, and his tongue did the most wicked things to her until her world began to spiral out of control.

Passion built inside her until she screamed. "Tanner!"

And he gently bit her, bringing her to a climax unlike anything she'd ever experienced.

With a gasp, he laid her back on the bed and then reached for his pants.

Before she could catch her breath, he was tearing open a foil packet and covering his penis in the protective shield. He gazed down at her, his emerald eyes glazed with passion as his fingers once again teased her until she finally grabbed his buttocks and pulled him into her.

"I need you now," she cried out urgently. "Deep inside me."

He smiled down at her. "Darling, I aim to please."

"Yes," she said as the spirals of desire reignited. She guided him with her hands on his buttocks as they found each other's rhythm. His mouth covered hers in a kiss that left her gasping for breath.

There was such a connection between them that with every thrust, he grew closer to her heart. With every thrust, she fell more in love with him and that was dangerous.

They both had been hurt by life, and she feared getting hurt, but at this moment, if he broke things off, she'd be devastated.

But there was no way she could stop what was happening between them.

With an urgency she'd never expected, they moved together, the bed squeaked, the headboard banged against the wall, but she didn't care. All she cared about was Tanner.

He lifted her hips until they were pounding away at each other, the rhythm building inside her until she feared she would explode. Every single thrust made her want him forever.

He gasped, and she let herself go once again as the world tilted around her. "Tanner."

"Oh, Emily," he said with a final jerk before collapsing on top of her.

When he rolled off onto the bed, she lay there, slowing coming back to earth, wondering why she'd never had anything like this with another man. Why had Tanner been the only one to make her world explode?

"That was great," he said.

"Yes," she replied. "Let's just hope it doesn't get us fired."

Laughing, he pulled her against him, his lips kissing her cheeks. "I don't care. It was well worth getting fired over."

She ran her hand down his cheek. "Thank you for saving me today. It seems we like to save one another."

Tanner's eyes narrowed as he gazed at her. "You're right."

"And tomorrow we'll save each other from getting fired."

He laughed.

"Darling, as much as I would love to spend the rest of the night in your arms, I think I should go back to my cabin. Don't want to tempt Aunt Rose too much."

With a sigh, she knew he was right.

"I agree, but can I have another five minutes? Today was scary and I need to feel the safety of your arms tonight. Hold me, make me feel that tomorrow everything will be all right."

"We have nothing to worry about, Emily." Leaning down, his lips covered hers. "You can have me again."

"Good," she said. "Once is never enough with you. I think I need you twice tonight."

CHAPTER 20

Later that night, Emily crawled into bed, exhausted. Tonight, she'd felt closer to Tanner than ever. There was no denying she was falling in love with him and that frightened her. Just thinking of him, her heart warmed, and she hugged the pillow where he'd lain.

His smell was on the pillowcase and she sighed.

It had been an exciting day, and she was ready to turn out the lights.

Suddenly lavender filled the air and she groaned.

Eugenia.

"Dear, are you all right? I saw what happened and I was so afraid for you. But my grandson saved you."

Oh my, had Eugenia helped that bull escape? No, she would not have put so many people in danger. Would she?

"I'm fine, Eugenia, but we need to talk. I know what you did."

The air shimmered with her appearance and the old

woman looked surprised. Emily knew she was faking the expression. She was certain that she'd been the one who sent Tanner into his episode.

The time to confront her about what she'd done was now. But Emily also worried that she might have had something to do with the bull. Just the way she reacted was enough to make her suspicious.

"You dropped that pan in the kitchen on purpose because you knew it would send Tanner into an episode. You overheard us talking about pretending to be going along with your matchmaking schemes and so you got even."

The ghost tossed up her hands in the air like that was the most ridiculous thing she could have said.

"Why on earth would I do that? I don't want my grandson even thinking he's back in the war. I want him thinking about you."

Oh yes, she most definitely started his episode.

"Which achieved your purpose. I think you heard us talking about you and you wanted to see how I would react to his hallucinations. Did I pass the test?"

The old woman laughed. "Why would I want to make my grandson have one of these 'episodes,' as you call them. I want him to be happy. Going back to a war, even in his mind, is not good."

The ghost was as stubborn as they came and crafty as well. Someday Emily was going to read up on the family history and learn her story. She wanted to know what else she'd done.

"Unless it achieved what you wanted. Which was for

the two of us to get together. You thought it would force us together and it did."

The ghost smiled. "You two are so cute together."

There was no doubt in Emily's mind that Eugenia had dropped that kitchen pan. She'd smelled the lavender right before the pan dropped. The woman didn't respond to her, she just sat there grinning.

"Did you stick around long?"

"Oh no, dear. When the clothes start coming off, I've accomplished—"

Emily started to laugh and shook her head. "Yeah, just what I thought. You accomplished your goal and then you got out of there before you witnessed us having sex on the floor."

A flurry of sparkles filled the air and she had to look twice to make certain that Eugenia was still there.

"Dear, you don't talk to your grandson's grandmother about the two of you having sex," she said. "It's not proper."

"You told me that you wanted to make certain that the family continued. I would think that would be exactly what you wanted to hear," Emily said, sitting up cross-legged on the bed. "Would you like to know that we did it that day without birth control?"

The ghost shook her head. "Birth control? Whatever are you talking about?"

Emily should have known better than to mention that, but she liked to test the woman's knowledge occasionally.

"It's a way to prevent the woman from getting pregnant. Your job is going to be a lot tougher now that there is birth control."

Swirling around, she sank down into a chair. "These old bones hurt when I stand too long. Now, tell me about birth control. Is there a way for me to get rid of it?"

Like Emily would tell her that information. She just wanted to plant some doubts in her mind.

Emily smiled. "I don't have enough time to speak to you about birth control. I need to get some sleep. I have breakfast to cook in the morning and then there is a meeting with Aunt Rose. You may have gotten us fired tonight."

The woman laughed. "Rose knows better than to cause my grandsons problems. I'll not accept her messing things up."

Emily tilted her head. "Please tell me you didn't have anything to do with that bull getting loose tonight."

"Dear, you need your rest. Tomorrow night, I think you should tell me about controlling births."

"Eugenia," she said in a warning voice.

She started to disappear and Emily yelled. "You have got to stop these shenanigans to push us together. Someone is going to get hurt."

"Sleep well, dear," Eugenia called as she disappeared.

Just what she didn't need, a matchmaking ghost asking about birth control.

But they did have sex in the kitchen that day without using a condom. It had been spontaneous and urgent and, oh dear, what if she was pregnant?

Warmth filled her. It would be their child, their baby, and she would love it, even if Tanner didn't.

For now, she would have to wait and see.

CHAPTER 21

Tanner went up to his Aunt Rose's office in the administration building. Years ago, she had an elevator installed and moved her office upstairs where she could look out over the ranch.

It was one minute after eight and she stood waiting for him by the door.

"You're late," she said.

"Not really," he told her. "My watch shows I'm right on time."

"Take a seat," she said, going behind her desk. She sank onto her chair and her eyes narrowed at him. "How did that bull get out yesterday afternoon?"

With a sigh, Tanner knew she would be upset about the accident, but he had never seen anything like that before. It was almost like the boards just broke apart as the bull approached.

"People could have been hurt. As it is, I'm going to have

to write up a report on the damage he caused. I want to know what happened."

This was not what he expected her to talk to him about today, but at least it wasn't about Emily.

"As a family member and a person in charge of the rodeo arena, I expect our guests to be safe watching the bull riders, even the calf roping and barrel racers. Never do I want to see a guest have to run for their life."

None of them did. Yesterday had been an anomaly. The oddest thing he'd ever seen happen with a bull. Never had he seen a bull escape from an arena that way.

"Neither do I," Tanner said. "We always check the fencing to make certain it's secure before every rodeo. The only way for an animal to get through the fencing is to do what that bull did yesterday. And that's the first time I've ever seen that happen. The boys said he ran all the way back to the pasture before they caught him."

His aunt Rose leaned back in her office chair and glared at him like what happened yesterday was all his fault.

"Don't let it happen again," she said.

"Like I could stop it," he said. "Our men acted swiftly to keep the people safe. They immediately went in search of the bull. They kept everyone from leaving, except you, and they warned anyone on the grounds to take cover. What else could we have done?" he said, growing agitated.

Their safety plans for just such an event had worked perfectly. What more did she want?

Forming a steeple with her fingers, she glared over her hands at him like she really wanted to take him down.

"Then there is this issue of you and our chef. I thought I warned you to stay away from her."

Oh hell, she was not going to let yesterday go. He'd saved Emily from the bull and yet she wanted to focus on their relationship.

"You did," he said. "Emily and I have come to an understanding."

Her eyes widened and he knew she didn't like his comments at all.

"Well, you may have, but I have not. I don't want this hot romance to end and my chef deciding to leave," she said, getting up and limping over to the window. Years ago, she had been injured in a horseback riding accident, and since then, she walked with a limp or used a cane.

"So I can't see Emily. I can't date her."

"My sources say you're doing a little more than dating," she said. "And no. I don't need this happening. It's a distraction. Our cook should be focused on creating excellent cuisine for our guests, not dillydallying with you."

"Your sources," he said, wondering what she'd been told.

"A kitchen floor is not private," she said.

How the hell had she learned what they'd done that day in the kitchen? There must be a camera somewhere in there. Who all had seen him and Emily at their most vulnerable? During a private moment. Thank God, they had remained mostly clothed.

"Did you enjoy watching us?" he asked.

Turning from the window, she frowned.

"You must have cameras in there because that's the only way you would have learned what went on."

She didn't respond, but he could tell she was growing angry.

With a sigh, he knew she would never understand what happened that day, but he had to try for Emily's sake.

"It just happened. I had an episode, and the next thing I knew, I was kissing her. She helped me come back from the battle I was in, and for that, I'm grateful. Things got carried away."

The woman's face grew red. "Until this moment, I wasn't certain it was true. But now I know what was told to me was real."

Crap, that meant one of his cousins must have viewed the footage and told her. Those nosy sons of bitches. Why had they not come to him?

"This is a business. Not the Love Boat or Fantasy Island or even the Dating Game. You may be family but you're also an employee. What you did is against the rules in the employee handbook. Page twenty-seven to be exact. We could be sued for sexual harassment."

Tanner just sat there and let the woman yell at him, his anger growing by the minute. He wanted that footage erased immediately. And he would find out which cousin had seen it and they were in so much trouble.

Because they liked to stir up shit.

"And then last night, you went inside her cabin. What the hell happened in there? You are fornicating with the employees," she said. "It was bad enough that your brother

Travis and Samantha hooked up. Do you men know how you endanger our livelihood?"

"Yes, ma'am," he said, trying to keep the sarcasm out of his voice.

"Keep your penis in your pants. If I catch the two of you again, I'll be forced to let Emily go," she said. "As for you, after the bull incident and this little fiasco, two weeks suspension. One for each transgression. Get off the property for two weeks. You're lucky I'm not firing you."

Stunned, he stared at his crazy old aunt. The woman was a hard ass. "Don't fire Emily. I'll go, but I don't know if I'm coming back."

Rising from the chair, he was shaking with anger. "Oh, and by the way, the ghost you keep trying to hide from the guests. Well, she is not going to be happy with you. She's been playing matchmaker with me and Emily. In fact, I expect she'll be serenading you tonight with her singing. Sleep well."

Tanner turned and walked out the door. If he found out which cousin had seen them in the kitchen, he better hide. Right now, Tanner was so mad, he all but stormed out of the building.

Walking across the yard to his cabin, he saw Travis coming toward him.

"We've got to talk," he said. "You're not going to believe what's happened."

"Yeah, we need to talk," Tanner said, thinking he was so over being a Burnett and working at the ranch.

"Samantha is pregnant," Travis said, a grin spreading across his face. "She took the test this morning because she's late and hasn't been feeling good. She's pregnant. We're going to have a baby."

Tanner tried to push aside his anger. This was what his brother needed. A new woman and a baby. Pausing in his stomp across the yard, he patted his brother on the back.

"Congratulations," he said. "I know how much this means to you."

"I'm so damn happy," Travis said. "Samantha makes me so happy. But this is wonderful."

Damn, now he hated to tell his brother what had just happened. He didn't want to ruin his good day but he had to tell him.

"You deserve this," Tanner said, remembering how much Travis had gone through when his first wife and child had been killed.

There was a perpetual grin on Travis's face, and Tanner knew his bad news would end that feeling of joy he was experiencing.

"We're getting married just as soon as we can. I was wondering if you'd stand up with me. Tucker has already said he would. But I really would like both of you."

"Of course," Tanner said. "Did you guys plan on her getting pregnant this quick?"

Travis smiled. "Not at all. We forgot to use a condom one night and here we are. One time and we're expecting a baby."

Like a slam to the gut, Tanner remembered.

One time. Only one time. Dear God, only one time.

The memory of them under the table, no condom anywhere near them, suddenly hit him. Damn, that little incident had caused nothing but problems. What if she were pregnant?

If he wasn't fit to be a husband, how in the hell would he ever be fit to be a father? What was he doing? This was nuts. He was crazy for thinking about having a relationship with Emily.

Maybe Aunt Rose was right. Maybe he was jeopardizing everything by being with Emily.

"What did you want to talk about?" Travis asked, gazing at him in a quizzical way.

Starting to stomp across the yard again, he realized they were halfway to his cabin. Halfway to the place he had to vacate for two weeks.

"Aunt Rose suspended me for two weeks, because of the bull yesterday and the fact that someone told her about Emily and me in the kitchen."

"What?" Travis's eyes widened.

"Yes, I've got to get off the property for two weeks," he said. "Guess who is going to get all the work. Because you know most of our cousins are way too lazy to do ranch work."

"I'm not going to be far from Samantha's side. I'm not doing all the work. That's bullshit," Travis said.

"You're damn right it is. But I want to know who saw me and Emily and ratted us out."

Travis shook his head. "That crazy old woman can be a real pain in the ass. Maybe she should take care of the guests."

With a sigh, Tanner reached the porch of his little cabin.

"I've got to pack my things and speak to Emily. I'm ending it. I'll never be a fit husband, and if we were to somehow create a baby like the two of you, that would be bad. I'll never be a good father."

He turned and started to walk off. Travis grabbed him by the arm.

"Don't do this, Tanner. You're just reacting to Aunt Rose. Give it some time. Don't break things off with Emily. She's good for you. These last few weeks, I've seen you doing so much better."

Pulling his arm from his brother's hand, he shook his head. "I've got to. For her own sake. Good luck, brother."

CHAPTER 22

Emily finished putting away the leftover breakfast food. The guests had enjoyed her eggs benedict and pancakes for those who didn't like the first choice.

This morning she'd never been happier. Last night had proven to her that she loved Tanner. She'd finally accepted that though she would have never planned to get involved with a military man again, life had put them on a path together, and she accepted the challenges that his PTSD would bring.

Together they could break this curse he was afflicted with, and she had no fears of the future. In time, when he was ready, he would ask her to marry him and she would say yes. It was all a matter of timing. Finding the right opportunity when they both felt comfortable pledging to spend the rest of their lives together.

This morning before she went to meet with Rose Burnett, she had baked Tanner's favorite cake. She had the time this morning and she wanted to do something special for him.

After she poured the strawberry gelatin over the cake, she topped it with whipped cream and then placed fresh strawberries on top. It was gorgeous. There was one for the guests and one she'd made just for him.

He deserved it after he'd saved her last night.

She would place it in the cooler and let it sit for several hours before she served it tonight.

Until then, she hummed as she cleaned up the dishes. So far, she was glad she'd made the move to Texas. The heat was daunting, but as long as she had air conditioning, she was all right.

The door to the kitchen swung open and Tanner came marching in. The glint in his eyes was dark and angry. Something was wrong.

"Good morning," she said, smiling at him, wishing her hands were not in soapy water so she could kiss him, try to ease the tension she saw in his face.

"We need to talk."

"All right," she told him, drying her hands.

Pacing the kitchen, he glanced at her.

"I'm ending it."

"Ending what?" she asked, wondering what had him so agitated. Had the meeting with Aunt Rose been that bad?

"I'm ending us," he said, glaring at her.

Astonished, she sank back on her heels, feeling like the world had just turned upside down.

"Why?"

Her chest ached. This had been her fear, her nightmare.

"You and me, it was a big mistake."

Shaking, she turned to him. "What has happened to make you act this way. Last night you…"

"You need to leave," he said, glowering at her.

Something had to have happened to make him act this way. They were back to her leaving again and that just irritated the hell out of her.

"Please, Tanner, tell me what happened. I thought that we were falling in love," she said.

For a moment, his eyes lightened, and then he shook his head.

"No. Everything was a mistake. You were just a fling that lasted way too long. Get out, go away. Go back to Colorado. You don't belong here. I'm never going to have anything to do with you ever again. I will do my best to get you fired. Anything to make you leave."

A rush of pure white anger filled her. She glanced around the kitchen where she had hoped to spend a lot of time and realized that, no, she couldn't stay. Obviously, something had happened and he wanted her gone. Now. Today. And she couldn't stay if she loved him and he hated her.

"As it is, my Aunt Rose has suspended me for two weeks because of you."

"Me? What did I do?"

"Yes, you," he said, staring at her, his face red and contorted with rage. "She knows about the kitchen. She knows about us in your cabin. And she does not approve. It's against the employee handbook rules on page twenty-seven."

The thought of someone watching them in the kitchen mortified her. Yes, she had to leave. She couldn't stay.

Stepping back from the sink, she walked to the table and picked up the cake.

"I don't understand what's going on with you. I don't know why she would suspend you because of me, but I'll give you a reason to fire me."

She carried the cake to him and smashed it into his face.

"A little something I made just for you this morning. Now you can wear it."

Turning on her heel, she removed her apron and hung it up by the back door. She was done. Time to find some other place. Time to get away from the crazy Burnetts.

CHAPTER 23

Shaking Tanner wiped the best-tasting strawberry cake he'd ever had from his mouth and face. Licking his fingers, he sighed. What if he'd just made a big mistake?

Had he been right to break it off with Emily? Or was he letting his Aunt Rose persuade him?

Didn't it serve his Aunt Rose right that she was losing her best cook? Now, instead of losing just him, she was also losing Emily.

Taking the towel, he rubbed the dessert off his face and clothes. His heart ached with the knowledge she would be leaving. No more kisses, no more laughing until they were rolling on the bed. No more late-night talks or cuddling.

Emily had been the closest he'd come to happily ever after and that's what frightened him the most. Just the thought of her accidentally getting pregnant was enough to make him end it all. He wasn't cut out to be a husband or a father.

There was no way he would endanger people he loved.

Desiree walked in. "Where's Emily?"

"She just walked out," he said, realizing that this was going to cause quite a stir at the dude ranch today.

"Oh, good, I can catch her still," Desiree said as she pivoted to run out the door.

"You better hurry, she's leaving," he said.

With a halt, she turned back to him. "Why are you wearing cake? What are you talking about?"

Standing there, he was ready to confront her. Only two people could have known that they were having sex in the kitchen.

"I'll answer your question if you'll answer mine," he said. "Did you tell Aunt Rose that Emily and I were having sex under this table?"

Desiree's face made an ugly expression. "What? Eww. No."

"Would you have any idea who would have said something to her?"

"No," she said, her face scrunching up. "Did you guys…"

"Yes, we did," he said. "You and Travis walked in right after it happened. I had just had an episode and she comforted me. Then we started kissing, and the next thing I knew, we were having sex right there."

He pointed to the table.

"That's crazy," Desiree said. "This is where our food is prepared."

"Yes, it is," he said, knowing that Emily would have cleaned the whole place very well.

Staring at him, she shook her head. "What have you

done, Tanner? Why would you break it off with her? She was the best thing that's happened to you in a long time."

That's what Travis said, and it was true, but he was too afraid. First, his Aunt Rose threatening him, and then Travis's news sending him over the edge. He had to end it with Emily for their own good.

"Aunt Rose suspended me and told me not to see Emily any longer, that I was risking us being sued for sexual harassment."

Desiree started laughing. "Are you kidding me? Don't you realize she's just jealous? Sometimes she gets a mean streak in her, and I swear, it's like a demon takes over. So you came over here and broke it off with Emily, who proceeded to smear a cake that looks absolutely delicious on your face."

"Yes," he said. "But Aunt Rose also told me that someone told her that we did it in the kitchen. You and Travis were the only ones who came in when we were cleaning up."

She shook her head and stared at him.

"It wasn't me. Uncle James checks the footage from cameras once a week. But I didn't think there were cameras in here," she said. "Have you told Emily?"

"Kind of," he said. "I knew it would send her running, and it did."

"Tanner," Desiree said, "you and Emily are good together. Reconsider what you're doing. You've been happier than I've seen you since before you left for the war."

It seemed that his entire family, except Aunt Rose,

seemed to think he was making a mistake by ending the relationship. His heart ached. It would be hard to get over Emily, but it was for the best. This way she wouldn't get fired because he could not keep his hands off her.

This way they wouldn't risk taking a chance and her getting pregnant. This way he wouldn't ask her to marry him and endanger her.

Only, his heart was breaking into a thousand pieces. And once again, he had to contain his hurt and not let anyone know how all of this affected him. Once again, he had to go into his fox hole, wherever that would be, and hide.

"I'm sure she's packing if you want to say good-bye, but it's over."

He turned to walk out of the kitchen and saw a tiny black camera on top of the cabinet.

"Damn, there it is," he said.

Grabbing a stepladder they kept in the kitchen, he climbed up and yanked the thing out of the wall. His Aunt Rose and Uncle James would not be spying on the next cook. And every time he found a camera, he would be removing them. Spying on employees was not good practice and he was going to tell everyone there were cameras around the place.

After climbing down the ladder, he walked over to the trash can and tossed it in.

"Good riddance," he said.

"I'm going to go tell Emily good-bye," Desiree said. "And tell her that my cousin doesn't realize what he's doing. That he's lost his mind."

"Oh, I realize very well what I'm doing. I'm saving her from being stuck with a man who still fights battles. I'm saving our children from being ashamed of their father. I'm doing the right thing for everyone."

And it hurts like hell.

Desiree turned and walked to the door. "And you're the biggest idiot on the planet for letting the one person who could help you leave. Be alone. You deserve it. You're making a huge mistake."

With a slam of the kitchen door, she walked outside. Standing there, he glanced at the floor under the table, his resolve weakening. Maybe he was wrong.

Suddenly the speaker in the kitchen went off. "Travis and Tanner Burnett come to my office immediately."

It was Aunt Rose, and he was not going. He'd been to her office once today, and if she wanted to speak to him, she could come find him. Obviously, she'd learned that Emily was leaving.

Wasn't this what his Aunt Rose wanted? The two of them to be separated. Well, they were certainly split, and now, it would be miles between them, not just buildings.

No, he was doing the right thing, breaking up with Emily, but why did it feel so bad?

CHAPTER 24

"I hate men," she said, pulling out her suitcases from under the bed. "All men. Even dead men. One dies and leaves me alone and the other is the biggest coward on the planet."

Opening the luggage on the bed, she started throwing her clothes inside. Tears hovered behind her eyelids. She was done. Finished.

Why had he done this?

Why?

What happened to have him suddenly withdraw completely from her? To decide that she was not the one he wanted to spend forever with? They had agreed to take it a day at a time, and she felt confident that eventually they would marry.

But suddenly everything was wrong.

And why didn't his aunt Rose want them to be together? She remembered her appointment with her and thought to hell with it. The old witch could learn like everyone else that she wouldn't be there. She would be fired, and right now, she didn't care.

All she could think about was getting out of here.

Never seeing Tanner again.

Never getting involved with a military man ever again.

She yanked open the drawers to the chest and pulled out her underclothes. Quickly she threw them in the suitcase. She just wanted to get out of here before someone tried to stop her. Anyone.

The smell of lavender filled the air.

"No," she cried. "Go away. You've caused enough trouble."

Eugenia shimmered into view and Emily turned away from her. Never again could she think of a ghost without remembering this apparition. And she no longer feared them.

"Dear, what's wrong? What are you doing?"

"I'm leaving," she cried. "You can have your grandson. I hope you get all those babies you want, but it's not going to be with me."

There was a moment of silence and then a puff of lavender was aimed in her direction.

"Stop and take a deep breath," Eugenia said. "Tell me what's happened."

Emily whirled around, thinking she would hate the smell of lavender from here on. "Where should I begin? Aunt Rose suspended Tanner for spending time with me, so he came to the kitchen and he broke up with me. Told me to leave. That I was nothing more than a one-night stand that had lasted way too long. So I quit. I'm packing and I should be out of here within the hour."

The ghost floated up and hovered right in front of her. "Rose has been a problem since her boyfriend broke up with her fifty years ago. The woman is a crazy old maid who doesn't believe in love. She thinks she's a career woman, whatever that is."

A chuckle escaped from Emily. She could see Rose believing that, but these people were all crazy and she feared if she stayed, she'd become just like them. Irrational.

"Well, good for her. I think she's onto something," Emily said, going into the bathroom and getting her things. "She suspended Tanner for two weeks."

The ghost made a growling noise. "She's not going to get any rest until my grandson returns. But you can't leave, dear. Don't you realize he cares for you? He's reacting because he's scared. Something sent him over the edge today."

"Well, he has kicked me to the curb and I'm going."

She snapped the suitcase closed and sat it on the floor. Then she picked up another bag and began to fill it with her personal items. The cookbooks she loved, her phone charger, and even a few novels she'd brought to read. Everything that was of any importance, she threw in the bag.

For a second, she wondered if that job in New York was still available. Not the quiet life she'd imagined, but they had a great reputation. And she wouldn't have to worry about being accused of sexual harassment or have to deal with a relationship with PTSD.

"Yes, I know he's reacting because he's scared. This has not been a walk in the park for me either. I understand, and believe me, I feared getting involved with someone who had the same disease as John. But I did. I fell in love with him and look where that got me: a one-way ticket out of here. Thank you, Aunt Rose."

Eugenia's wings spread wide. "You can't leave him if you love him."

"Sometimes love is not enough," Emily said. "Sometimes the person you love has to be willing and able to accept your feelings. And if they can't reciprocate, then there is no point in continuing."

"Did you tell him you loved him?"

Why would that have made a difference? This morning, he'd been determined to end it with her. Nothing she said would have stopped him. She'd even mentioned that they were falling in love, but that hadn't slowed him down. He wanted her gone and she was going to grant his wish.

"No, it would not have changed anything."

"You don't know that for certain," Eugenia said.

Oh, yes she did. Nothing would have changed his mind.

Emily finished packing and glanced around the room. She'd enjoyed staying here. It had been a great job, except for the fact that she'd fallen in love with Tanner.

"The problem is not with me," Emily said. "The problem is with Tanner. I don't even know what brought this on today. Last night, everything had been perfect. We made love and yet, this morning, he was a raving madman determined that I leave."

A knock resounded at the door. Desiree walked in. "I

know what brought this on today. I can explain to you exactly what happened."

A tall, beautiful woman walked into the room behind her. "Hi, we haven't met. I'm Travis's fiancée, Samantha. Hello, Eugenia. I'm so glad you're here."

"Darling, if I could hug you, I would," the older woman said.

They were a little late. She glanced at her watch. She wanted to hit the Dallas-Fort Worth traffic before rush hour.

"Nice to meet you. I'm Emily and I'm just about to leave. I wish we could have gotten to know each other better."

The woman walked over and sank down into the chair by the bed. "Sorry, but I've been so tired lately. Desiree and I have pieced together what happened and want to explain to you what we think caused Tanner to end it with you so abruptly. You need to know."

Emily gazed at the two women. "How did you piece it together?"

"It's a timing thing," Desiree said. "First, Tanner had that awful meeting with Aunt Rose that even now we're trying to get reversed. She gave him a two-week suspension. So he was very upset about that."

"Travis was not too happy about it either," Samantha said. "That puts all the ranch work on him."

Eugenia floated into the air. "I'm going to make that woman's life miserable tonight. Why did she suspend my grandson?"

Desiree laughed. "The bull incident at the rodeo yesterday and then her seeing Tanner and Emily together."

Eugenia was quiet and Emily turned to her. "You had something to do with that bull getting out, didn't you?"

The ghost sighed. "Well, I just thought how wonderful it would be for my grandson to rescue you. Save you. I thought it would help him to realize how he's falling in love with you."

"You caused that?" Desiree asked, her eyes widening. "No wonder he's so pissed. He didn't do anything and yet the bull got out and he took the blame for it."

"Well, it did bring them together," Eugenia said sheepishly. "It was for love."

"You haven't learned, have you," Samantha said. "You can't be in control of getting people together."

One thing Emily hoped she didn't have at her new job, wherever that could be, was an interfering ghost. Especially a matchmaking ghost. Just thinking it made her feel crazy.

"What else happened that caused Tanner to break it off with me?"

"This was the hardest part to figure out," Desiree said. "But when I ran into Samantha today and learned her news, it made sense."

Samantha grinned. "Travis went to speak to Tanner this morning. He asked Tanner to stand up with us. We're getting married a little quicker than we planned. I'm pregnant."

"Thank you, Lord," Eugenia said, fluttering around. "I'm so happy. Another Burnett. Another grandson or granddaughter. Just what this old woman needed to hear. My matchmaking is working."

"Oh, please," Desiree said.

"Congratulations," Emily said, her heart beating in her chest. But why would that send Tanner running from her? She didn't understand.

Desiree smiled. "After you left the kitchen, I came in. Tanner told me that he would not be a good husband or father. He didn't want to embarrass his children. Evidently when Travis told him Samantha was pregnant, he worried about you getting pregnant. He still doesn't believe in himself."

Oh dear, she could be pregnant at this very moment. But this all seemed so farfetched.

"Well, ladies, while I think you're right, it doesn't change things. He wants me gone. He told me to leave, that I was just a hookup that had lasted too long. So I'm going to load up the bug and I'll be leaving."

Desiree hugged her. "I'm so sorry. You're perfect for him and he's too stubborn to see it."

"Don't give up," Samantha told her. "It took me and Travis splitting up before we realized how we'd made a huge mistake. It still could happen."

Emily wasn't going to hold her breath. She was walking out of here and moving on.

"Eugenia, better luck next time," Emily told her. "One thing you've accomplished is that I no longer fear ghosts. As long as they're as good as you are, then I have nothing to fear."

"We'll see each other again," Eugenia said. "For now, I've got work to do."

She swirled out of sight and Emily felt the tears spilling down her cheeks. It was over and now it was time for her to go.

"Good-bye, ladies. And good luck with the baby," Emily said, thinking of how she could possibly be pregnant at this very moment.

But Tanner would never know. If he didn't believe he was good enough to be a husband and father, she would not push him.

And she deserved a man who wanted her. Someone who promised to be a good man who loved her with all his heart.

Loading up her yellow bug, she glanced around at the ranch one last time before she climbed behind the wheel. Time to move on.

CHAPTER 25

Tanner had grabbed a suitcase, and this time, he was filling it with T-shirts and jeans and anything he wanted to wear. He would leave for two weeks, and hopefully, if he returned, the memory of Emily would be gone. If not gone, then at least erased to some degree, or maybe he would never return.

He was tired of trying to meet the demands of Aunt Rose while the rest of his cousins skated by. Enough.

Travis knocked on the door and entered.

"You're making a huge mistake," he said.

"Yes, well, it's my mistake to make," he said as he continued packing.

None of them understood his plight. None of them realized the danger he posed to them. None of them knew how the episodes were physically and mentally draining. And when he returned from one, he often lay there in a stupor willing it all to go away.

No woman deserved to be with a man like that. Especially Emily. Sweet Emily. When he'd learned about Travis and Samantha's unplanned pregnancy, he knew he had to end it with Emily.

Still he worried she could be pregnant. They had unprotected sex and he could not risk being near her again. He would not make a good father. He could not keep his hands off her.

"Please, don't go off and leave me. You know the other cousins don't work near as hard as we do. I need you here to help with the dude ranch. Tomorrow night is the finale for this week and we have to prepare for a new round of guests on Sunday."

"Nope," he said. "Maybe she can help you. She can make certain the horses are saddled and ready to ride. She can clean out the horse stalls or maybe even show them how to hold a roundup. Oh, and be sure to let her run the rodeo. She can keep a mad bull from charging the fence. Take it up with Aunt Rose."

He'd had enough.

"What are you going to take up with Aunt Rose?" the old woman said.

They both turned and she was standing there inside his small cabin. Just what he didn't need.

"Did neither one of you hear the announcement to come to my office," she said.

"I heard it and ignored it," Travis said.

"I'm packing to get off the property for two weeks just like you said," Tanner replied, done talking to her.

Travis all but growled at the woman. "And I think I'm going to leave for two weeks because you know as well as I do who will have to take care of both his job and mine. You can get one of the cousins to do both of our jobs for once," Travis said. "Including running the rodeo."

She walked farther into the room, her cane thumping on the wooden floor. "Sounds like I have a mutiny on my hands."

"Push me any further and I will not return," Tanner said. "I'm done."

"If he doesn't return, I'll be leaving. Don't need the money I make here. It's only to help out the family. Samantha and I could travel a while before we settle down."

Suddenly the smell of lavender filled the air and Tanner moaned. Just what he didn't need. The ghost that had caused so much trouble.

"Eugenia," Aunt Rose said. "It's been many years since I've seen you."

"Rose," Eugenia said, drawing out her name. "I hear you don't like sleep."

"What are you talking about?" Aunt Rose said, frowning.

"You suspended my grandson, you've prohibited him from seeing Emily, and basically broke them up, and interfered with my matchmaking," Eugenia said, her voice growing louder. "Oh, and that damn bull escaping yesterday was because of me. I wanted my grandson to rescue Emily, hoping it would make this stubborn boy realize how much he was falling in love with her. But these Burnett kids are just as stubborn as my boys."

Rose frowned. "You caused the bull to crash through the fence? Did you not think of the danger to others?"

"Yes, I did," Eugenia said. "He wasn't going to hurt anyone. That poor cow is scared to death of me. So he ran, all the way back to his pasture."

"You could have hurt someone," Rose said. "That was a dangerous stunt to pull."

"No one got hurt. I would not have let them."

"So what has all of that got to do with my sleeping?"

Eugenia started singing off-key. "Buffalo gals, won't you come out tonight. Come out tonight. Come out tonight." The ghost cackled. "You're going to be hearing that all night long for causing my grandson so much grief. Emily has packed up her stuff and she's just about to pull out."

"What? No," Aunt Rose said, all but running to the door.

"Oh, yes, when you broke them up, she decided she'd had enough. Plus, my grandson broke her heart. He also told her to leave. So she's gone. Thanks for interfering, Rose. You really don't want the family line to continue, do you?"

"Of course, I do," she said.

The ghost swirled from one end of the room to the other and Tanner recognized it was a sign she was furious.

"Then stop interfering with my matchmaking. You did that once before and look where it got you. An old maid."

Aunt Rose's face turned red, and she raised her fist at Eugenia. "You old witch, I'm going to call a ghost hunter and have them get rid of you."

"Just try," Eugenia said. "I'll pull you into the grave with me."

Aunt Rose took a step back. "Emily has left?"

"Yes," she said.

"Damn it, she was the best cook our kitchen has ever had. Finally, I thought we were going to serve some fine cuisine. Finally, something besides barbecue," Aunt Rose said.

Tanner closed his suitcase and started for the door.

"Stop," Aunt Rose said. "This morning, I was feeling mighty cranky."

"Just because you caused so much heartache," Eugenia asked. "You need to wake up in a better mood. But your mood won't improve for a while. Buffalo gals, won't you come out tonight," Eugenia sang.

His aunt Rose stomped her cane on the floor and leaned her hands on the wooden top.

"Look, I'm sorry about suspending you. Travis and Tanner, I know you two run the dude ranch. The others are window dressing, but you are the ones who always make certain the guests are taken care of. I was wrong to suspend you, especially now that I've learned how that damn bull escaped. And Tanner, you and Emily butted heads from the first time I saw the two of you together. But if you want to be together, I won't stand in your way."

"Nope, she's gone," Tanner said, anxiety filling him instead of relief. What in the hell had he done?

"Oh good grief," Travis said. "You love Emily, and you're just too damn stubborn to admit it. She's the only one who has helped you. Damn, man, don't give her up."

Tanner felt tears well in his eyes. He did love Emily. All morning, he questioned what he'd done. All morning, he tried to believe he was doing it for her good, but he needed her.

"I'm just afraid. What if she gets pregnant? You're going to be a great father. But me, what are my kids going to do with a father who every so often goes wacko?"

Travis smiled and shook his head at his brother.

"Kids adapt. They will love you for who you are. They will understand," Eugenia said. "Your namesake experienced problems when he came home from the war and his wife and children were his everything. It will be the same with you."

"Did he ever get over what the war did to him?"

"It took him awhile, but his lovely wife helped him, and they had a long happy life together," Eugenia said.

Did he want Emily to leave?

No, he wanted Emily here by his side. He ran out the door and looked for her yellow bug sitting outside her cabin.

It was gone.

Just then a tractor pulling a load of hay backfired, the noise sounding like a hand grenade. The walls of the ranch disappeared and he was thrust back into the war zone. Combat raged around him and his best friend Brandon was beside him.

"This is crazy," Brandon said. "We're outnumbered two to one."

"But they don't have the same type of firepower we have," Tanner told him.

"Oh shit, they have missile launchers. Take cover," Brandon screamed.

Tanner flung himself down onto the ground. “Someone get that missile launcher!”

Rising, he aimed his rifle, just as the tube launched a heat-seeking missile. In fewer than ten seconds, it landed not far from them, shaking the ground.

“Here comes another,” Brandon yelled.

Tanner picked up his walkie-talkie. “We’re taking missile fire. We’re surrounded and not looking good.”

“Roger, Sergeant. Air cover has been ordered.”

“Look out,” Tanner screamed, the missile landing too close. His ears rang.

Travis grabbed Aunt Rose. “Call the gate and tell them not to let her leave. Tell them Tanner is having an episode and we need her here to help us. Now.”

CHAPTER 26

Tears streamed down her cheeks as she drove up to the guard house, where the man stepped out in front of her bug. "Ma'am, Miss Rose Burnett asked that you please return to Tanner's cabin. He's having an attack."

Staring at him, she wanted to say too bad. But couldn't do that to the man she loved. No matter what happened between them, she had to help him.

"All right," she said. "I'll turn around."

The man stepped out of her way and she steered the yellow bug around the guard shack and headed as fast as she dared to Tanner's cabin.

Was he really having an episode or was this just a way to entice her to stay? Right now, she knew she could not stay here working at the ranch if they were not together. She didn't need a proposal, but she needed to know this was just not some stunt to get her to stay.

She pulled the car to a halt in front of his cabin, turned

it off and jumped out, leaving her purse, her keys everything ready to go.

Racing up the stairs, she entered the house and saw the others standing around watching in horror. The furniture was turned over and a lamp was smashed on the floor. Tanner crouched behind a side table, eyes wide with fright. His arms held his imagined gun at the ready, and he was shouting.

"Get down. James, to your left. Hit that son of a bitch," he screamed.

Whirling around, he gazed at the wall, then dove backward, taking out the sofa table. "Incoming."

Down on the ground, he crawled, and she moved in.

She sang to him and he cocked his head in her direction. Then slowly she ran her fingers down his cheeks and he turned to her touch. "Come back to me, Tanner. Come back to me, love."

She sang a soft lullaby, and she knew the moment she reached him, his body sagged against her.

"It's over. The war is over and you're safe. Your men are safe. Stay with me."

Leaning his head against her shoulder, he reached up and pulled her mouth to his. Like a starving man, his lips covered hers and he drank from her. From the place of safety.

It was like that day in the kitchen when passion had overcome them, but this time, she leaned back until their lips came apart.

"Are you all right?"

"Yes," he whispered, staring at her. "Don't leave me."

Surprised, she leaned back and stared into his emerald gaze that was unwavering. "You wanted me to go. You told me I was a hookup that—"

"You are a one-night stand that I want to promise forever to. Stay by my side until death parts us," he said, gripping her face with his hands. "I need you."

"What about children? You're afraid your PTSD won't make you a good dad. I don't believe that for one moment," she said, gazing at him. "You're afraid it won't make you a good husband."

With a sigh, he pulled her into his arm. "It's not going to be easy. I'm a damaged man. But you know how to help me through these episodes. You know how to calm me. How to make me feel safe. I don't want to be a failure. Our children deserve a good father and mother. I'll do the best I can."

Tears welled in Emily's eyes. "And I'll do the best I can to be a loving wife to you who helps you every time you have one of these episodes. Our children will also help you. They'll grow up knowing what to do."

Emily's heart soared, but he had yet to say those words she needed to hear. The words she knew promised her forever. Waiting patiently, she clung to him. What if he didn't say them?

"Emily, until you left, I didn't know how much I needed you. How much I had fallen in love with you. Marry me?"

A grin spread across her face as she held onto him tightly. "Yes, I'll marry you. I love you, Tanner. What we have is special. Don't ever forget that."

The people in the room clapped, and it was the first

time Emily really noticed they were there. She'd noted people when she walked in but didn't realize who all was there.

Aunt Rose, Travis, and his new fiancé Samantha stood watching them.

Samantha walked over. "What if we had a double wedding? Two of the Burnett brothers marrying at the same time. We could hold it outside here at the ranch. What do you think?"

Tanner glanced up and smiled. "If Emily is okay with the idea, I would love it."

"I love it," Emily said, thinking it would be so different from her first wedding.

Aunt Rose stood back and shook her head. "What a great idea. Is Eugenia still here?"

The ghost floated into view. "Of course, I am. I'm so happy. Another Burnett boy is getting married. Two at the same time."

"I hope this means I'm going to get to sleep tonight?" Aunt Rose said. "After all, we did bring them back together."

"*I* brought them back together," Eugenia said bluntly. "There was no *we* in this. Only me. Now, if you'll excuse me. I have to do some reconnaissance work on my next grandson. Time to start working on number three. And don't you even think of interfering." She pointed a finger at Rose. "Toodles."

The apparition shimmered as she disappeared.

"Grandson number three?" Travis said and then he

started laughing. "That's going to be a hard shell to crack. Tucker is married to his work."

Tanner helped Emily to her feet, but he kept his arm around her and Emily was glad. She needed to feel a connection with him.

"If you people will excuse us, Emily and I are leaving for the weekend. We're going back to the hotel where we met and we're going to spend the weekend getting to know one another without all you people around."

Aunt Rose's eyes widened. "But what about the kitchen? I need a cook for tomorrow night."

Emily was not about to argue with Tanner. She liked his idea.

"Barbecue," Travis said. "We'll serve them barbecue."

"And I'll help," Samantha said.

Together, hand in hand, they ran out the door. Emily stopped to grab her purse and packed suitcase. Tanner had grabbed his bag. They hopped into his truck and Emily reached over and squeezed his hand as they pulled out of the ranch.

While she had not planned on finding love here in Texas, love had found her. And she was forever grateful.

CHAPTER 27

Tanner took his bride's arm and they followed Travis and Samantha as they walked down the makeshift aisle to the justice of the peace standing at the front of the tent, waiting on them.

He was getting married to the love of his life and he was so excited. The girls had worked together, and here they were getting married almost two weeks to the day since he'd proposed.

Glancing at Emily, he smiled. No, they hadn't known each other long, but she was the woman for him. So far, he'd not had an episode since that day, and he hoped with her help, they would continue to be fewer and fewer.

She was late. It was still too early to tell, but he was starting to get enthusiastic about the thought of a baby. The cousins would be so close in age and he knew how Burnett cousins loved to get into trouble together.

They arrived at the officiant and Tucker stood beside the man along with Desiree. Both girls had agreed that she should be the person standing up beside them, and he was thrilled.

"Dearly beloved, we are gathered here today…" the man said.

Five minutes later, it was over, and to the claps and cheers of the crowd, he kissed his bride while Travis kissed Samantha.

They were married.

After the photos, they went to the reception hall where there was a sit-down dinner. Toasts were made to their happiness and then they had their first dance together as man and wife.

"Do you remember our first dance?" he asked her.

"Of course, I was dancing with this handsome man and wondering how I could get him into my room."

He grinned. "And I was wondering how I could get you to let me into your room."

"Oh, Tanner, I came to Texas not looking for a husband but to start over. I found not only love with a good man, but an entire family."

"Who will probably drive you crazy," he said.

She laughed. "To think that a ghost brought us together is rather strange."

"A matchmaking ghost."

Just then the lights blinked on and off and the music stopped. Everyone glanced around the room.

"Tucker, grandson, you're next. It's your turn to find love."

"Go away, Eugenia," Tucker called. "I'm not going to marry. You're wasting your time."

She laughed. "Oh, I love a good challenge. That's what all the Burnett men say. As for the rest of you, get ready, I'll be coming for you after Tucker. The family must continue."

With a sparkle of lights, she disappeared and the music began again.

Emily shook her head as she gazed at her husband. "Poor Tucker has no idea what he's up against."

"Oh, I think he does. But he won't win."

"No, he won't," Eugenia said with a whisper around them. "Now I'm ready for some grandbabies. Get to work."

They both looked at each other and laughed. "What she doesn't know won't hurt her. I did a pregnancy test this morning, Tanner."

His heart started to pound in his chest. "And?"

"Baby Tanner will arrive in about eight months."

Joy filled him.

"And you're going to be a great father."

"I hope so. I truly hope so," he said and pulled Emily in close. "Let's blow this joint. I'm ready to spend some time in your arms celebrating."

"Agreed," she said.

They ran out the door before anyone could stop them. They didn't need the bird seed thrown at them for good luck. Tanner would do everything in his power to make their union happy, and Emily would too.

* * *

THANK you for reading Tanners story. I must admit this couple fought me on every page. They were not an easy couple to bring together, but in the end, I did love their story. You can help an author by leaving a review. Next up is Tucker. I can't wait to share his adventures with you.

The Bodyguard, The Actress, and the Matchmaking Ghost

Texas billionaire Tucker Burnett keeps his international acclaimed security business and personal life separate even when he's protecting the world's most beautiful women. When his client is almost killed, he takes her to the only place where he knows she'll be safe – his family's ranch – and hopes his ancestral ghost behaves herself.

Madison Wood is the biggest star in Hollywood, but she's got a secret. Someone wants her dead. When her handsome bodyguard whisks her away to the boonies, she's more than a little miffed. Especially, when he gives her exactly what she needs.

When she leaves the lure of Hollywood behind, the Burnett ghost insists that Madison can have the family she's always longed for with the man who would lay down his life for her, but can she give up the life of luxury and fame to be a rancher's wife?

Does their love have a ghost of a chance?

Available Everywhere!!

Jennifer Moss is having a really bad day.... But it's about to get even worse...

Her teenage son's grades have plummeted. Her husband is distant and cold, and now she's received a letter from the child she gave up for adoption twenty-five years ago.

But a knock on the door, spins her world out of control.

Losing everything, she packs up and returns to Mustang Island where the secrets from her past slowly unravel.

And the boy she left behind so many years ago helps her see that this new beginning could be the best thing that's ever happened to her.

But will their secret child unravel their relationship before it has a chance to begin again?

At Your Favorite Retailer

Contemporary Romance

Burnett Brides Contemporary Times

Travis

Tanner

Tucker

Joshua

Jacob

Justin

Cameron

Caleb

Cody

Desiree

Burnett Brides Contemporary Box Set Books 5-7

Burnett Brides Contemporary Box Set 8-10

Burnett Brides Contemporary Box Set 11-14

Return to Cupid, Texas

Cupid Stupid

Cupid Scores

Cupid's Dance

Cupid Help Me!

Cupid Cures

**Cupid's Heart

Cupid Santa

**Cupid Second Chance

Cupid Charmer

Cupid Crazy

Cupid's Bachelorette

Cupid Games

Return to Cupid Box Set Books 1-3
Cupid Help Me Box Set Books 4-6
Return to Cupid Box Set Books 7-9
Return to Cupid Box Set Books 10-12
**The Unlucky Bride

Contemporary Romance
My Sister's Boyfriend
The Wanted Bride
The Reluctant Santa
The Relationship Coach
Secrets, Lies, & Online Dating

Bride, Texas Multi-Author Series
**The Unlucky Bride

Coming Home for Christmas
I'll Be Home for Christmas
White Christmas
Santa's Baby
All I Want For Christmas
Box Set

Inheriting An Irish Groom
Inheriting a Scottish Castle

Kissing Oaks Billionaire Brothers
The Cowboy Billionaire's Lucky Break
The Cowboy Billionaire's Fate
The Cowboy Billionaire's Playbook

The Cowboy Billionaire's Secret
The Cowboy Billionaire's Deception
The Cowboy Billionaire's Match
Kissing Oaks Billionaire Brothers Box Set 1-3
Kissing Oaks Billionaire Brothers Box Set 4-6

Lipstick and Lead 2.0
Nailing the Hit Man
Nailing the Billionaire
Nailing the Single Dad
Box Set

Secrets of Mustang Island
Secrets of a Summer Place
Secrets of a Runaway Bride
Secrets From the Past
Secrets of a Reckless Life
Secrets of a Hidden Life
Secrets of a Midnight Letter

Secrets of Mustang Island Novellas
The Summer I Loved You
When We Meet Again
Christmas at Mustang Island

The Langley Legacy
Collin's Challenge

Short Sexy Reads
Racy Reunions Series

Paying For the Past
My Christmas Soldier
Cupid's Revenge

Western Historicals
A Hero's Heart
Second Chance Cowboy
Ethan

American Brides
**Katie: Bride of Virginia

Angel Creek Christmas Brides
**Charity
**Ginger
**Minne
**Cora
Angel Creek Christmas Box Set

Bad Girls of the West
Scandalous Sadie
Ravenous Rose
Tempting Tessa
Nellie's Redemption
Bad Girls Box Set

The Burnett Brides Series
The Rancher Takes A Bride
The Outlaw Takes A Bride
The Marshal Takes A Bride

The Christmas Bride
Boxed Set

Lipstick and Lead Series

Desperate
Deadly
Dangerous
Daring
Determined
Deceived
Defiant
Devious
Lipstick and Lead Box Set Books 1-4
Lipstick and Lead Box Set Books 5-9
Lipstick and Lead Box Set Books 1-9
**Quinlan's Quest

Mail Order Bride Tales

**A Brother's Betrayal
**Pearl
**Ace's Bride

Scandalous Suffragettes of the West

**Abigail
Bella
Mistletoe Scandal

Southern Historical Romance

A Scarlet Bride

The Cuvier Women
Wronged
Betrayed
Beguiled
Boxed Set

The Debutante's of Durango
The Debutante's Scandal
The Debutante's Gamble
The Debutante's Revenge
The Debutante's Santa
Box Set

** **Denotes a sweet book.**

Want to learn about my new releases before anyone else? Sign up for my New Book Alert and receive a complimentary book.

Sylvia McDaniel is a USA Today Bestselling author with over one hundred western historical and contemporary romance novels under her belt. Known for creating memorable bad boys and good girls who can't help getting into trouble, she spends her days weaving compelling tales filled with heart, humor, and unexpected plot twists. Her family-oriented stories have earned her a loyal fanbase, and she's always dreaming up new ways to keep her readers turning the page.

Married to her best friend for over thirty years, Sylvia lives in Colorado, where she enjoys hiking and taking in the natural beauty of the forest that borders their home. Their spoiled dachshund, Zeus (who has his own column in her newsletter), and brat dog Bailey keeps them company on their adventures.

Sylvia keeps close ties to her southern roots, especially when it comes to football. A dedicated fan of both the Denver Broncos and the Dallas Cowboys, she's happiest when they're winning.

Love books? Love deals? Love a little mischief? Sign up for my Substack—it's free!

https://sylviamcdanielauthor.substack.com/

The End

www.ingramcontent.com/pod-product-compliance
Lightning Source LLC
Chambersburg PA
CBHW061229170626
46809CB00007B/2579

* 9 7 8 1 9 5 0 8 5 8 8 2 8 *